FRANKIE FiSH

AND THE KNIGHTS OF KERFUFFLE

ALSO BY PETER HELLIAR

Frankie Fish and the Sonic Suitcase

Frankie Fish and the Great Wall of Chaos

Frankie Fish and the Viking Fiasco

Frankie Fish and the Sister Shemozzle

Frankie Fish and the Wild Wild Mess

Frankie Fish and the Tomb of Tomfoolery

Best Ever Pranks and More!
(written by Frankie Fish & Drew Bird)

PETER HELLIAR
FRANKIE FISH
AND THE KNIGHTS OF KERFUFFLE

Art by
LESLEY VAMOS

Hardie Grant
CHILDREN'S PUBLISHING

Frankie Fish and the Knights of Kerfuffle
published in 2021 by
Hardie Grant Children's Publishing
Wurundjeri Country
Ground Floor, Building 1, 658 Church Street
Richmond, Victoria 3121, Australia
www.hardiegrantchildrenspublishing.com

All rights reserved. No part of this publication may be reproduced, stored in a retrieval system or transmitted in any form by any means, electronic, mechanical, photocopying, recording or otherwise, without the prior written permission of the publishers and copyright holders.

Text copyright © 2021 Peter Helliar
Illustration copyright © 2021 Lesley Vamos
Series design copyright © 2021 Hardie Grant Children's Publishing

Series design by Kristy Lund-White
Illustrations by Lesley Vamos

A catalogue record for this book is available from the National Library of Australia

Hardie Grant acknowledges the Traditional Owners of the country on which we work, the Wurundjeri people of the Kulin nation and the Gadigal people of the Eora nation, and recognises their continuing connection to the land, waters and culture. We pay our respects to their Elders past, present and emerging.

Printed in Australia by Griffin Press, part of Ovato,
an Accredited ISO AS/NZS 14001
Environmental Management System printer.

1 3 5 7 9 10 8 6 4 2

The paper this book is printed on is certified against the Forest Stewardship Council® Standards. Griffin Press holds FSC® chain of custody certification SGS-COC-005088. FSC® promotes environmentally responsible, socially beneficial and economically viable management of the world's forests.

FOR MY GRANDPARENTS:
AILSA & BERT. VIN & KITTY.

A SHORT BIT BEFORE WE FIND FRANKIE FISH

An old man with a hook for a hand turned and sighed in his bed, while his wife, an ex-nurse, patted his forehead with a damp cloth.

'How are you feeling now, Grandad?' asked his granddaughter warmly from a nearby chair.

The old man smiled weakly back. 'Much better, Louise. For a while there, I didn't know if I was Arthur or Martha.'

'Well, you're Alfie now, thank goodness,' his wife said as she took his temperature.

'That's right, my Mavis. I'm *yer* Alfie.' He beamed.

Alfie Fish had been in the hospital again, following another spell where he was very muddled and extremely fuddled. Fortunately he was home now, but unfortunately these spells were getting worse and more frequent, as Alfie was not only very old, but 'struggling with memory problems', as Nanna sometimes put it. The doctors called it Alzheimer's disease.

Frankie Fish – Alfie's grandson – called it **unfair**. He was determined to find a cure. Frankie and his best friend, Drew Bird, and his sister, Lou, had even travelled back in time to seek help, using the Sonic Suitcase that Grandad had invented. Months had passed since they had returned from the Wild West via St Mary's Hospital in Glasgow, and for a while the recommendations of eating more vegies and fruit and doing regular exercise had helped a little. But no-one lives forever, and it seemed that Alzheimer's was finally getting the better of Alfie Fish.

'Need anything before I go?' asked Lou, getting up from her chair.

'Actually, yes,' Grandad said, with a rare look of clarity in his eye. He shuffled along the bed to sit up a little.

Lou and Nanna shared a look before leaning in. 'Let me guess, you want haggis for lunch again?' Lou grinned. 'I'm not sure we should after the *smell* last time ...'

But Grandad was distracted, and his fingers were fidgeting with the blanket. He clearly had something weighing on his mind.

'What is it, love?' asked Nanna Fish, suddenly worried.

Grandad took a breath. 'I think it's time,' he said. 'Time we **destroy the Sonic Suitcase**.'

The announcement hung in the air for a few seconds as Nanna and Lou tried to work out if this was Grandad talking, or the Alzheimer's spruiking another crazy idea. Like a week earlier, when Grandad had announced that he wanted to wear a ball gown to the shops, or the day before, when he believed that bananas were spying on him.

'Oh, why's that, love?' asked Nanna softly.

'Yeah, Grandad, I thought you loved learning

about history and getting into the odd life-threatening adventure,' offered Lou.

Grandad finally looked up. 'No doubt we've had a lot of fun with the Sonic Suitcase, and, yes, there have been plenty of scrapes. Oh, the scrapes!' His eyes twinkled as he paused, recalling their many misadventures. 'But the suitcase was never supposed to be used as long as it has been, and I'm not going to be around forever to keep fixing it after every bang and bungle. In fact, I barely have enough time to teach ye half of what I know, Lou ...'

Lou's eyes were filling with tears, so Grandad cleared his throat and patted her hand. 'The thing is, if the suitcase **breaks down** while one of us is using it, we might never be able to get home. That'd really mess about with our timelines,' he said, in what was definitely the understatement of the century, 'and it might also muck up the history of the **entire world**. And we can't risk that.' He paused to gather his thoughts. 'I know we've been very lucky up until now, but sooner or later luck runs out for all of us. So it's time to put the suitcase to rest. OK, my dears?'

For a moment, Lou could only nod. She could see in Grandad's eyes that this was *him* talking, not his ailment. And she knew he was right – luck was indeed a fickle thing.

When she found her voice again, she had only one question. 'Who's going to tell Frankie?'

Grandad looked at Nanna, who looked at Lou, who looked back at Grandad. Clearly nobody wanted to volunteer. It'd be like volunteering to tell a cat that mice had been completely eradicated, or a dog that there were no more bones in the world. In other words, it was probably going to go *very* badly.

And indeed, how Frankie Fish would react to having his beloved Sonic Suitcase destroyed *could* change the history – and the future – of the world. How, you ask? Well, you'll simply have to read on to find out …

CHAPTER 1

SHOW OFF AND TELL

Lisa Chadwick's face beamed like the headlights of a monster truck. Frankie didn't know WHY he always had an almost allergic reaction to Lisa whenever she took centre stage, but he did. His chest would tighten, his palms would sweat, and his stomach would churn like it was preparing butter for a toast-obsessed army.

'This clarinet has been in my family for over eighty years,' Lisa proudly declared. She pulled on a pair of delicate white gloves before gently taking the old instrument out of its elegantly weathered case. 'My great-grandmother would play it every night for months while she waited for my great-grandfather to return from the war.'

'Maybe that's why he took so long to return!' Drew snickered, and then quickly went quiet when Miss Merryweather shot him an ominous look.

Luckily, one of the Mosley triplets began armpit-farting a sad military tune, which drew the teacher's attention away from Frankie Fish's best friend.

Waving her gloved hands in a very annoying fashion, Lisa announced that she was the *only* person permitted to handle the precious Chadwick heirloom. She held it aloft and walked around the room, smacking the hands of anyone who dared encroach on the clarinet's personal space.

It was the first annual Celebrate Family

History month at St Monica's, so during Show and Tell the students were taking it in turns to present their most impressive family heirlooms to the class. Kimmy Klute proudly read out the picture books her dad had written when he was a boy, while Harry Chen carried in his great-great-grandparents' very large and very serious-looking wedding portrait, in which you could see his great-great-grandad's extra left thumb quite clearly. Very cool.

The Mosley triplets had brought in their extra-large, extra-thick jar containing **ancient farts** passed down by generations of stinky Mosleys. Way less cool.

'Legend has it,' said one triplet (who knows which one), 'that if you open the jar without adding a fart, the ones inside will leap out and GRAB your –'

'That's QUITE enough, thank you, Mosleys,' Miss Merryweather groaned, before calling on Lisa to present her boring clarinet.

The only thing stopping Frankie from projectile vomiting during Lisa's presentation was knowing that, as old as her family's clarinet was, Drew had her beat.

Well. And. Truly.

Drew and his dad had recently become interested in their ancestry, and had managed to trace their roots all the way back to Indian merchants in the spice trade centuries earlier. So when Miss Merryweather had excitedly announced that everyone needed to present a special object from their family's history, Drew knew exactly where he wanted to go and what he wanted to do when he got there. Yep, he wanted to go back in time to collect an extra-special object from his ancestors – no surprises there. The surprising thing was that Drew wanted to do this on his own. Without Frankie, his very best friend. And so, with a nervous frog in his nervous throat, Drew had asked Frankie for an extra-special favour.

'Can I take the Sonic Suitcase for a spin ... by myself?'

At first, Frankie thought Drew was joking and responded with an immediate and thunderous guffaw. But when he saw his best friend's face staring back at him, a little hurt, he knew he was serious. **Deadly serious**.

Frankie didn't know what to say. They had always time-travelled together, which meant they always had fun together. It also meant they could get each other out of trouble. *And let's face it*, Frankie thought to himself, *it's often Drew who gets us into trouble in the first place.* What would happen if Drew got into a spot of bother without Frankie there to help him out? And, more importantly, why didn't Drew want Frankie to come along on this adventure? Didn't he like Frankie anymore?

'I need to do this, Frankie,' Drew had pleaded. 'It's not because I need to beat Lisa Chadwick, although that would be pretty cool. I need to do this for me. To prove something to myself.' He swallowed. 'I need to prove I can have an adventure ... without you there to lead the way.'

In the silence that followed, Frankie thought about a lot of things. He thought about how he *did* often lead them on their trips through time – and how he'd never considered how that made Drew feel. Once, Frankie had dragged Drew to clash with Vikings in Norway, en route to getting a genuine Viking outfit, just so he, Frankie, could beat Lisa Chadwick at the St Monica's Halloween costume competition. And he'd taken Drew to the Wild West to help find a cure for Grandad's memory problems – but they'd never done anything to help Drew or his family. Frankie hadn't thought about that before, but now that he did, he felt **AWFUL**. Drew had always gone along with Frankie's plans. Now he had been brave enough to ask Frankie for this favour – so it was Frankie's turn to go along with Drew's plans, even though that meant not actually going along with Drew on this particular adventure.

Frankie swallowed hard, doing his best not to look upset, and said yes.

Drew, naturally, was over the moon. 'I'll be super careful,' he promised, grinning. 'I'll wear the earpiece Saint Lou made so I can communicate with you while I'm away, and I'll be back before you know it!'

And that was how Drew time-travelled by himself with the Sonic Suitcase to the spice trade in the fifteenth century. Frankie tried not to think of all the fun Drew was having without him – and he definitely did *not* think it might mean Drew didn't want to be his best friend anymore. Not much, anyway.

Drew returned with a minimum of fuss. He came back with stories told to him (with the help of the suitcase's translating padlock, of course) by the merchants in his family: stories of travelling across the seas to bring strange and exotic spices to foreigners far and wide, and sleeping under the stars. It all sounded *very* exciting.

For the next few days Frankie kept a close eye on Drew, trying to work out if his best friend no longer liked him. But, since Drew didn't ask to use the suitcase on his own again, and seemed to be acting normal – well, normal for Drew Bird – Frankie told himself he just had to believe everything was OK, and that he and Drew would go on many more adventures with the Sonic Suitcase – together – for many more years to come.

Unfortunately, Frankie had no idea how wrong he was. But he didn't know that just yet.

Finally, it was Drew's turn to present his family heirloom, although Lisa Chadwick insisted snootily on continuing to take her clarinet around the room so that everyone could see it close up.

Drew didn't seem to mind, though. He got

up with a cheeky smile and placed a large, very old-looking wooden case on Miss Merryweather's desk. 'Today I'm showing you some of the ancient spices that my great-great-great-great-great – look, just trust me, they were *really* great – grandparents used to sell along the Silk Road,' he said proudly. 'I have ancient jars of cinnamon, cardamom, ginger, turmeric, pepper –'

Lisa snorted rudely. 'I have all of those spices at home too. That doesn't seem very special.'

Frankie groaned, but Drew insisted, 'No, no, these are the *original* spices! Come and have a smell, you've never smelt ANYTHING like them.'

Everyone bounded out of their chairs and crowded around while Drew delicately opened each jar. Finally the oohing and ahhing seemed to bother Lisa, and she huffily wedged her way to the front of the crowd, hissing, 'Shove over and let *me* have a smell!'

Gingerly holding her family's clarinet with one gloved hand, Lisa leant in to smell the jar of pepper at exactly the same time that a Mosley triplet leant in on her other side. Before anyone could stop him, the Mosley triplet took a huge sniff and quickly turned an alarming shade of purple. 'Ahhhh,' he huffed. 'Ah, ah …!'

And before Lisa could move her precious clarinet even an INCH out of the line of fire, the Mosley triplet exploded in the world's hugest, wettest, most peppery sneeze of all time – all over the clarinet, and all over Lisa.

'... **AH-CHOOOO!**'

Drew turned to Frankie and winked. 'I told you my trip would be worth it,' he said.

CHAPTER 2

FRANKiE HAS NOTHiNG TO SHOW AND NOTHiNG TO TELL

As Frankie walked home from St Monica's Primary that day, with Lisa's hysterical, pepper-laced screams echoing in his ears, he couldn't stop thinking about his own presentation, which was due the following week – right before the end of term. All month he'd been 'forgetting' to bring his family heirloom, but Miss Merryweather had finally laid down the law.

'Next week, Frankie!' she said, exasperated.

'Everyone in class has to do it, including you. And NOTHING in a jar, OK? I've had more than enough of jars this week.'

At this point, all Frankie had was a video of Grandad's favourite movie, *Braveheart*, and he knew that wouldn't be good enough. He couldn't take Grandad's old car-racing trophies to school – the last time he'd borrowed one for a school project, Grandad had called the cops every day for a week, convinced it had been stolen. *Think, Frankie!* he told himself. *You've got to have SOMETHING good.*

Of course, Frankie did have something rather special up his sleeve. Just as it had helped Drew, a certain **time-travelling suitcase** could be the answer to all of Frankie's problems, too.

When Frankie arrived at Grandad and Nanna Fish's house, he was greeted by his nanna, her arms reaching out like a friendly zombie to wrap him in a cuddle.

'Hi Nanna, is everything OK with Grandad?' he asked, squeezing her back.

'He's good, love! He's looking forward to seeing you, actually,' Nanna said lightly, cupping Frankie's cheeks in her hands before planting a big smooch on his forehead.

Frankie gently creaked Grandad's bedroom door open and popped his head in, hoping he wasn't about to wake Alfie up or spy him doing **nude aerobics**.

Luckily, Alfie Fish was doing neither of those things. He was sitting up in bed writing in a card that had a picture of forget-me-nots on it. *Probably writing to the local council to complain about noisy garbage trucks*, Frankie thought. Grandad did like to get rather **cranky** in letter form.

'Hi Grandad, had a good day?' Frankie enquired playfully.

'Kiddo,' his grandad smiled back, 'when ye

get to my age, if there is breath in yer lungs, it's a good day.'

As Grandad patted the bed, inviting his grandson to take a seat, something caught Frankie's eye: the Sonic Suitcase was resting on the doona. This was strange – usually, when it wasn't in use, the suitcase lived in the Forbidden Shed with the door firmly closed and locked. This was partly to stop anyone using it without permission, and partly so it didn't get damaged – although, Frankie noted as he sat down, the suitcase had seen better days. Who'd have thought that being speared by Olympic javelins, tossed in Viking mud and prised open by greedy town sheriffs was not good for luggage upholstery? Even with Lou's ongoing improvements – adding a rainbow lightshow here, or the translating padlock there – the Sonic Suitcase was certainly battle-weary, and the buckles didn't look as sturdy as they once had. Grandad was the one who really kept the suitcase in working order.

'Is everything OK?' Frankie asked as an uneasy feeling settled over him.

Grandad wasn't one to beat around the bush. 'We've had a good run, lad,' he said bluntly but not unkindly. 'It's been the most glorious roller-coaster of all time. But all roller-coasters have to come to an end.' He patted the bruised shell of their time-travelling suitcase and gave Frankie a firm look. 'I'm putting the suitcase out of action.'

'Already?' Frankie said, the blood draining out of his face. 'But – but – I'm not ready for this roller-coaster to end!'

'It's knowing the ride will eventually stop that makes the dizzying ups and the hair-raising downs bearable,' Grandad pressed on firmly. 'If the roller-coaster never stops then it's just madness. **Madness** and **chaos**. And it's my duty to keep ye safe.'

Frankie was speechless. Deep down, he'd

known this day would come, and yet he didn't feel he'd ever be ready for it. It wasn't just about using the suitcase to go find a family heirloom – although there was that. It was also that the Sonic Suitcase had made Frankie's life – and his family's life – so special. And he didn't want that to end.

'Truth is, I'm closing in on the end meself,' Grandad went on gruffly. 'And the suitcase is showing its age. It's deteriorating, just like my memory.' He cleared his throat, and Frankie had the distinct and bewildering impression his cranky but beloved grandad was trying not to cry.

Frankie took a deep breath. His grandad had trusted him with a lot over the past year, and he could see that this was hard for him to say. He also had the feeling that Grandad had made up his mind, and it would be almost impossible to get him to change it. But Frankie just had to convince the old man to let him have one more trip. One tiny trip to help with a school project. Just one little trip with Drew Bird, to prove once and for all that they were still best mates. And even if they weren't ... couldn't they have one last trip together, for old time's sake?

'I think ... I think I understand,' Frankie said slowly, trying to sound as grown-up as possible. 'But ...'

Grandad laughed. 'Talking to ye is like looking into a stable of horses.'

'Huh?'

'There is **ALWAYS** a **BUTT**!' Grandad chortled.

Frankie snorted. 'OK, but this is a good but!'

'Nanna always said I had a good butt,' Grandad snorted, never one to let a good opportunity pass.

Frankie groaned, trying to keep the image of his grandad's butt from his mind. 'No more butts!' he exclaimed. 'Grandad, I understand what you're saying. Do you think I could use it just ONE more time, though? Please? It's really important!'

With that, Frankie told him about Celebrating Family History month at school, and Drew's recent adventures with the spice merchants, and how it was apparently going to take three weeks for a specialist restoration team to clean all the pepper out of Lisa Chadwick's clarinet.

Frankie noticed Grandad's eyes losing focus as they drifted around the room. Occasionally he would say 'yes, yes' like he was listening, but Frankie wasn't sure that he was. By the time Frankie finished making his case to borrow the suitcase one more time, he felt rather disheartened.

'So I thought maybe I could go back in time to visit one of our ancestors and bring back something really cool,' he finished. 'Something that wouldn't stuff up the timeline of history, of course,' he added, knowing all too well the chaos that could happen if you took something from the past into the future – like the time he'd accidentally taken two Viking brothers into the present day. **Oops**.

Grandad's focus snapped back as he took in his grandson sitting dejectedly in front of him. 'Did I ever tell ye about the **Chalice of Flames**?' he asked.

'Um, no?'

'Yer great-great-great-great – give or take – Uncle Arthur was a knight in medieval England,' mused Alfie.

'Great!' shouted Frankie, a little too loudly. He paused. 'Wait. His name was Arthur? You mean, like, King Arthur and the Knights of the Round Table?'

'What? No, lad. Don't be daft. He was a butcher. And he was supposed to have bought some mystical chalice off a **witch**. There are other stories about it, but I don't know them –'

'Wow,' said Frankie, his mouth open wide

enough to fit an emu egg. 'Are witches even real?'

'Real or not, back then people believed in 'em and feared 'em,' Grandad declared. 'And I must admit I've always been curious to see that chalice, especially since Arthur apparently lost it in a **jousting match** and it was never seen again. Ye'd just have to find it before Arthur lost it, and bring it back. Would that work for yer Show and Tell?'

'YES! PLEASE! PLEASE! PLEASE!' Frankie pleaded. 'Let me go back and find it – just one more adventure – and then we can dismantle the suitcase together.'

Grandad rolled his eyes and gave a huge heaving sigh before finally saying, 'OK then, kiddo, ye have my blessing, but just be bloody quick about it.' Then a coughing fit took hold.

As Grandad sputtered and spluttered, Frankie stood up and retrieved the suitcase from the bed. He felt torn – he was both worried for his grandad and keen to get time-travelling one final time with Drew.

'Are you OK?' he asked as Grandad finally got control of his cough.

'I'm fine, lad,' Grandad said gruffly. 'Off ye go, then.'

But as Frankie headed for the door, Grandad added, 'Kiddo ...'

The old man had got out of bed and was standing there looking a little lost, like he wasn't quite sure if he was at the bus station or in the queue for movie tickets.

'Do you know the best thing that suitcase has given us?' Grandad said, his voice as wobbly as a trapeze artist with a fear of heights.

'Adventures and a front row into history,' Frankie announced.

A feeling of pride surged through him; he was sure he had said exactly what Grandad had wanted him to say. If this was an exam, he thought smugly, he would have received A++ for his response.

But to Frankie's surprise, Grandad was shaking his head. 'No, lad, there is something far more special.' His voice was breaking, just the tiniest amount. 'It's us,' he said softly. 'The suitcase gave us ... **us**.'

A warm glow spread through Frankie's chest, but he didn't know how to respond. He really wanted to hug his grandad, but they weren't really *huggers*, and he didn't want to make the old man grumpy. He wanted to tell him how much his life had changed since his grandad had allowed him into his secret time-travelling world. About how it made him feel like he was **special** – a feeling he'd never felt before. He wanted to say so much, but instead he said nothing as a lump the size of a cricket ball suddenly lodged itself in his throat.

Then Frankie did something he would regret for the rest of his life. Instead of giving his grumpy old grandad a hug, he just grinned at him and said, 'You're right. Us!' Then he added, 'You'll be here when I get back with the chalice, won't you?'

'I hope so, kiddo. I hope so.'

CHAPTER 3

A VERY WEIRD TRIP

Imagine being stretched ...

Stretched like your arms and legs are made of rubber spaghetti extended first across hemispheres, and then around planets. Your left arm extends around Mercury as your right hangs on to the rings of Saturn for dear life. Your legs cradle Uranus and Mars. The tiny Earth spins like a mirror ball around your body before disappearing into your belly button.

The whirling blue-and-green ball shoots

through a heavy fog of lint before navigating your internal organs. It's surrounded by red, echo-y digesting noises and goop. And then you realise ... you're inside someone's body.

Frankie looked at Drew. Drew looked at Frankie. They could hear each other's thoughts. *'Is it just me, or is this waaaaaay weirder than normal?'* Frankie thought, to which Drew thought back, **'*Waaaaayyy weirder!!!!!*'**

Suddenly, famous figures from throughout history started jumping out from behind organs. Marie Curie popped up from behind a kidney, Aristotle perched on the liver, and Adam Goodes was standing on the heart while Rosa Parks sang the Frank Sinatra classic 'My Way' on the gall bladder.

Eventually Frankie and Drew felt a suction-like pulling sensation, like whoever's body this belonged to was sucking on a vacuum cleaner (which you should NEVER do). *'Hold on!'* Frankie screamed in thought, and before they knew it they were being shot up through the throat and out of the thankfully open mouth like fish being fired out of a whale's blowhole.

It felt as if they were travelling at high velocity over many kilometres and even more years – until they came to an abrupt stop. They found themselves floating for a moment, then being turned around so they were facing downwards, and Frankie could not have believed his eyes even if they had been strapped to a lie detector – for below them was not the body of Frankie Fish, which he'd thought they were travelling through, but rather a colossal Grandad Alfie Fish.

'Er, did we just pass through your grandad?' Drew shouted, trying not to mind-vomit.

'Maaaaaaybe?' yelled Frankie, his eyes bugging out.

Grandad looked like a giant below them – like a Grandad version of the Marshmallow Man in *Ghostbusters*.

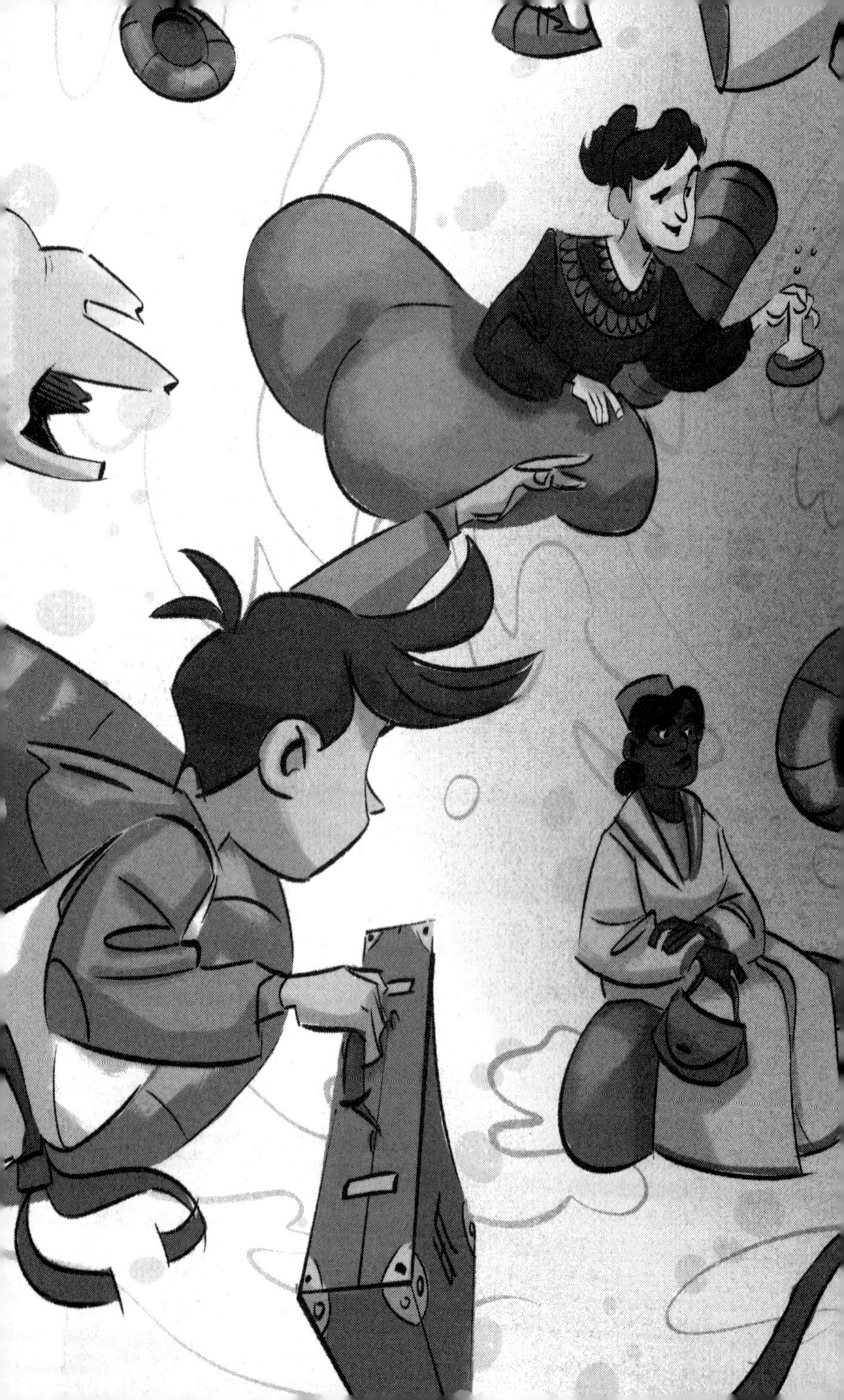

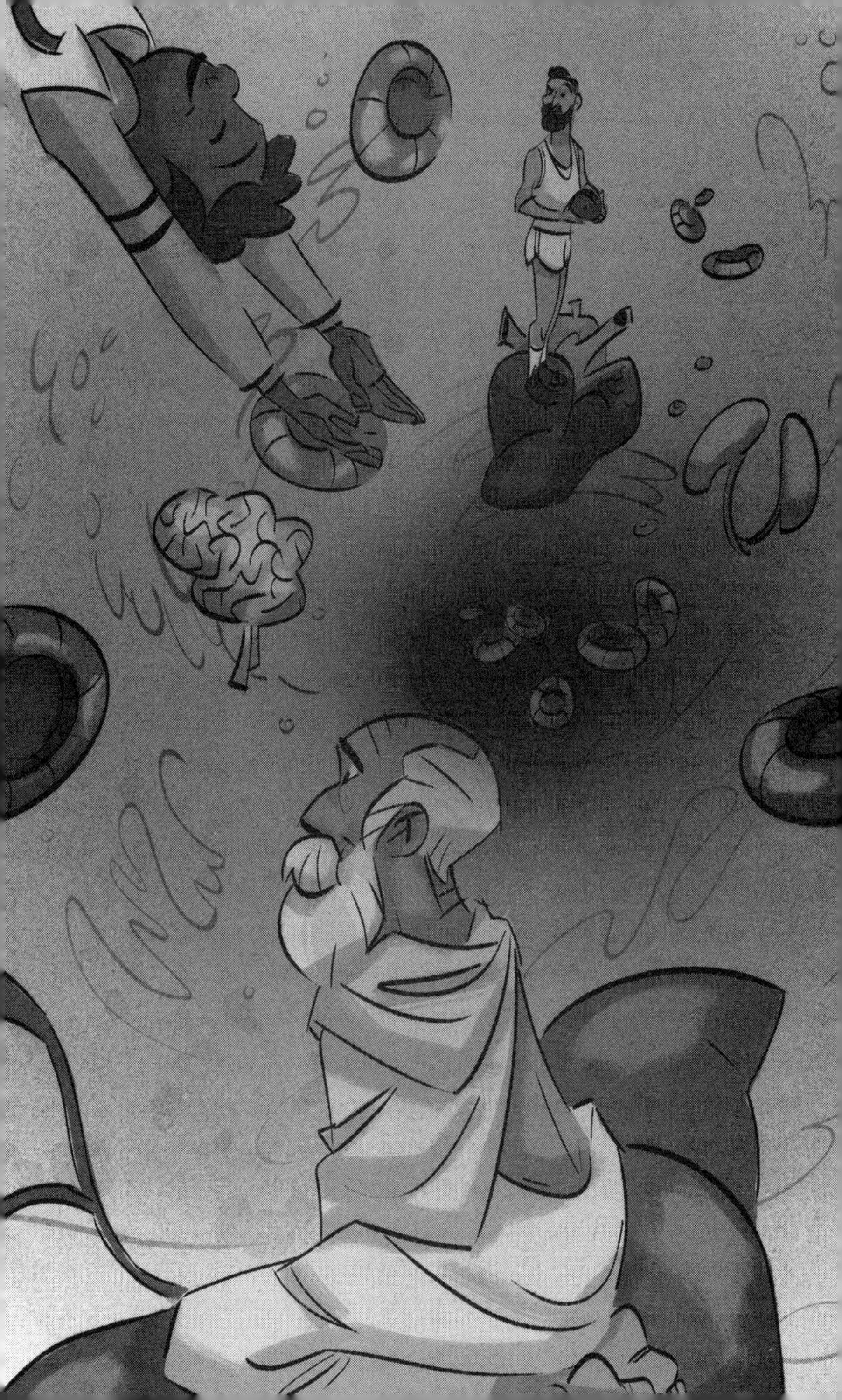

Frankie looked down into Grandad's eyes and heard him say, '**Be home soon**.' Then Frankie and Drew began spinning quicker and quicker.

'*Hang on,*' Drew's mind shouted, and before they knew it they were sucked back down and into Grandad's mouth.

To anyone else, this would appear totally random, but Frankie and Drew knew better. This wasn't random ...

This was time travel. For the **last time**.

CHAPTER 4

THE VILLAGE PEOPLE

Slushy snow mixed with thick mud, wood smoke and cow dung.

That's what Frankie Fish could feel and smell when he landed back in the Middle Ages. He just hoped the cow dung wasn't actually in the mud too. He gave it a quick sniff and was mightily relieved it smelt like regular mucky mud, perhaps with a delicate hint of straw.

He sat up, the squishy mud moving below him, relieved to see Drew was snoring alongside him in the same patch of sludge. Drew had a habit of sneaking in a nap whenever they took a trip back in time – he said he liked to be fresh for his arrival.

Frankie staggered up to standing, attempting to wipe the filth from one of his hands with the filth from the other and discovering that filth doesn't clean filth. He would need to find some water to help scrub the muck from his hands. Preferably running water. A fire hose would be ideal.

A fire hose seemed unlikely. Frankie shivered and stretched as he took in his surroundings. There were snowcapped mountains to his left. At the base of the hill he was standing on was a frozen river; pine trees flanked it like soldiers at Buckingham Palace. The river twisted and turned its way down to a village, where stone buildings were adorned with lanterns that glowed even in the daytime. Some of the buildings had spires that reached upwards, like children attempting to touch the ceiling.

'Are we there yet?' Drew Bird yawned, and then realised what he was lying in. 'PLEASE don't tell me this is **poo**?'

'I'm pretty sure it's not.'

'"Pretty sure" isn't good enough for me,' Drew replied, scrambling up like a jack-in-a-box who'd farted in his box. 'It's cold here!' he added.

Luckily, the boys had dressed for the occasion in double layers with hoodies on top, topped off with hessian sacks. They had each taken the belts from their fathers' dressing-gowns and tied them around their middles. Drew had pointed out to a reluctant Frankie that it looked like they were wearing hipster onesies.

Truth be told they looked **terrible**, but so did many people in the Middle Ages so they were sure to blend right in.

'Is that where we find Great, Great, Great, Great et cetera Uncle Arthur?' Drew asked, pointing towards the village.

Before they'd set off on their latest adventure – with their fingers crossed that it didn't turn into *misadventure* – Grandad had told them about the village where he thought they'd find the butcher's shop of one Arthur Fish, a Scottish pig farmer who, against the wishes of his family, had relocated to England to work in the meat trade.

'I hope so,' replied Frankie, picking up the Sonic Suitcase. 'It actually looks like a fairytale, don't you think?'

'I wouldn't know,' shrugged Drew, 'I'm more of a comic book kind of dude. Hey, let's slide down the hill to the river on our butts!'

So that's exactly what they did, giggling all the way until they landed on the muddy banks of the frozen river.

But, despite the laughter, Frankie couldn't stop thinking serious thoughts. He kept thinking about his last exchange with Grandad and how emotional the old man was. Frankie knew Grandad was getting older and closer to the end, but he didn't like to think about what that actually meant, and what life might be like without his beloved old cranky grandad. He was determined to find the **Chalice of Flames** before it was lost, and then get back to Grandad as soon as humanly possible.

'Let's clean up and get going,' said Drew, as if he'd read Frankie's mind. 'I'm starving. I hope your uncle's a good cook!'

Once the adventurers had wiped the muck from their hands as best they could, they set off towards the village. As they got closer, it looked like a postcard come to life right before their eyes – not just the vivid images of thatched huts and steam rising in the cold, but the mix of smells, too, which were both delicious and putrid. The delightful waft of baking bread, roasting meat and wood smoke was occasionally trumped by the stench of spoilt dairy, rotting animal entrails and human wee. It was a **lottery of smells!** Almost enough to give their twenty-first-century noses a complex.

Frankie and Drew were surprised by how vast the village was. Walkways shot off like octopus tentacles from the main town square, which hosted a large cathedral and many market stalls. The locals were a random mix of odours and sights. Some looked (and smelt) rather like Frankie and Drew, with dirty clothes hanging on by their final threads. Many of the men wore knee-length tunics, while others sported tight jackets and stockings. Some of the women wore full-sleeved, elaborately decorated dresses. They walked carefully and sometimes had to hitch their dresses up so they wouldn't drag in the muddy ground.

Frankie was staring at one such daintily dressed couple when he and Drew walked past a sign announcing:

> # LORD FARTHINGTON'S ANNUAL JOUSTING CONTEST
> ## - ENTRY 2 SHILLINGS -

'That'll be the jousting contest where the Chalice of Flames went missing!' Frankie said, nudging Drew. 'Maybe we should hurry up and find Great Uncle Arthur's butcher's shop. Last thing we need is to get sidetracked … um, what's that?'

At that moment, a knight with a **pig on a leash** walked past them. The knight was not exactly the fittest specimen around; soft bulges of flesh were visible through the gaps in his ill-fitting armour, and his helmet was crooked. Just as the pig wobbled past Drew, it emitted a rather pugnaciously foul fart.

'Well, that was a lovely welcome,' Drew muttered sarcastically as the pig's fat behind lurched away.

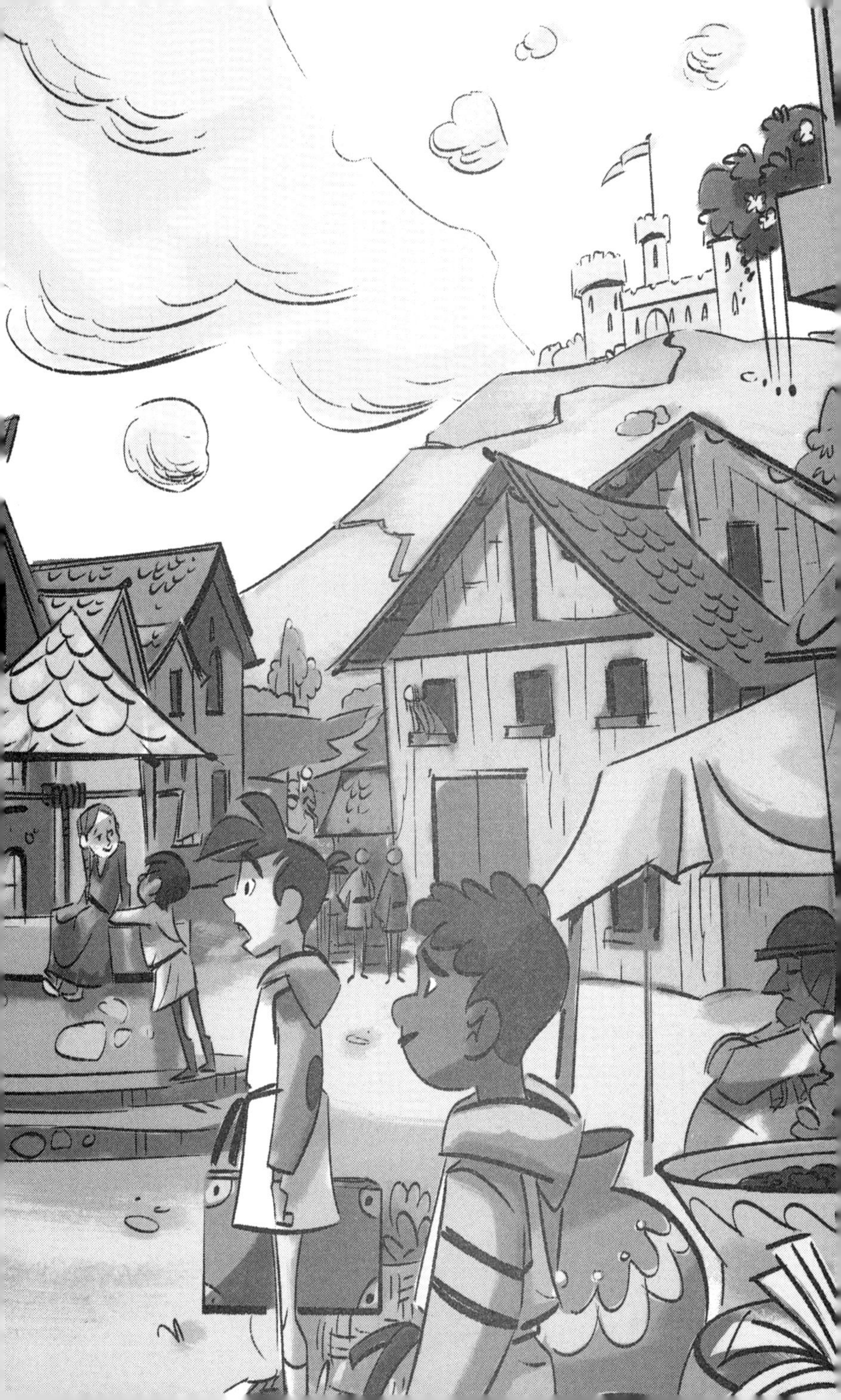

Frankie shook his head. 'Focus!' His eyes darted around the town square, thankful that the signs were in English on this trip. 'Blacksmiths, Worthington Stables, Keegan's Granary,' he read aloud.

'I don't suppose there's a Timezone, by any chance?' Drew joked, trying to shake off the smell of bacon-fart.

Frankie grinned. 'No, but look – there it is!' he shouted, pointing to the BUTCHR sign in the furthest corner of the square.

Frankie and Drew zigged and zagged past stalls selling everything from crates of chickens to bales of wool as they made their way across the noisy, crowded square. Every now and then someone walked by holding a tray laden with fragrant bowls of stew, shouting, 'Beef ribs!' and 'Cooked meat!' Drew licked his lips.

Frankie paused to watch some farmers herding cattle to a nearby livestock yard. Despite the ever-stronger stench of rotting animal parts, he couldn't help but smile – they'd only been in medieval England for five minutes and already they'd located his uncle's butchery!

But the smile quickly left his face when he saw a sign on the door that read in plain olde-worlde misspelt English: *CLOSD FREVER.*

'Um, I think it's meant to say "Closed Forever",' Drew piped up.

'Thank you, Sherlock Holmes,' Frankie said, groaning.

A lady was sweeping outside the bakery next door, and noticed the boys' despair. 'You just missed him,' she said kindly. 'Today was his last day in the shop – he's retired now.'

'Which way did he go?' Frankie asked impatiently. He didn't have a home address for Great Uncle Arthur, and if they didn't find him now it could send the whole mission into a pile of **pig poop**.

'That way,' she said, pointing back the way they'd just come from.

'Do you mind telling me what he looks like?' Frankie begged.

'You're not from around here, are you – everyone in town knows what Arthur Fish looks like!'

Frankie smiled. His uncle was a celebrity!

The woman raised her eyebrows, then said, 'You can't miss him – silly bugger came across a set of knight's armour a while back, and now he wears it all the time even though it don't fit right. Oh, and he has a pet pig. Walks it on a lead like it's a bloomin' dog. Be warned, they're as crazy as a bag full of wigs – Arthur AND his pig.'

CHAPTER 5

ARTHUR THE NOT-QUITE-AS-GREAT-AS-WE-HOPED

Drew couldn't believe it. 'Does that mean you're somehow related to that filthy animal?'

Frankie didn't have time to explain how family trees work – he had an uncle and a pig to catch. 'Come on!' he said, running back the way they'd come. He knew their targets had a head start, but surely it wouldn't be that hard to catch a pig being led on a leash by an old, fat man wearing steel cladding.

Frankie and Drew bounded out of the village, glancing left and right like clowns in a parlour game, but the pig and the knight were nowhere to be seen. Which meant they had to choose a direction: left or right?

'We could split up?' Drew offered, but Frankie shook his head. He was determined that he and Drew stick together, because that's what friends do – especially best friends, right?

'Right,' said Drew, and Frankie looked at him, surprised, until Drew added, 'or left?'

Left or right? Right or left? Should they head for the green hills with mossy rocks and boulders to the left, or back into town on the right? The sun was beginning to set over the frozen river.

Hurry!

'So?' Drew asked urgently.

Frankie tried to look as though he were giving the matter some serious thought, but really it was just a feeling in his gut that made him say 'left' and take off towards the hills. It was a fifty-

fifty chance and if Frankie could have crossed his toes while running, he would have.

Frankie didn't particularly *like* running with Drew because it reminded him how much faster Drew was than him. As his best mate leapt splendidly before him and the distance between them grew, Frankie found himself wondering if Drew could have won an Olympic medal during their recent trip to Ancient Greece.

As Frankie's legs grew heavy and his breath began to draw thinner, he heard Drew's voice call out from behind a large boulder up ahead. 'I found them! They're here!'

This put a spring into Frankie's tired legs, and he sprinted towards his friend's voice, swinging the Sonic Suitcase by its handle. As he rounded the corner, skidding on the dewy grass, he found Drew holding the pig by its leash. Uncle Arthur, the pudgy knight, had removed his helmet. He was sitting on a rock trying to catch his breath.

'I'll ... show ... 'em ... I ... will!' Arthur gasped.

He looked **furious** and it was quite clear that the two time-travellers had interrupted him in the middle of a monologue directed at the pig.

As the beast started to nibble curiously at Drew's feet, Frankie asked, 'Er, show them what, exactly?'

'Have you ever heard of jousting?' his great-great-great (you get the gist) uncle replied.

'I was wondering what exactly jousting was! Is it a board game? It sounds like a board game,' Drew Bird said.

Frankie shook his head. 'It's that weird game where knights on horses run at each other with telephone poles, right?'

Arthur's forehead crinkled. 'I have no idea what these ... telephone poles? ... are exactly, but you are basically correct. We call them jousting sticks. But apparently they will not allow me to enter Lord Farthington's Jousting Festival this weekend!'

'Is his name really Lord Farthington, or is it

Lord Fartington?' Drew smirked.

Frankie elbowed him. 'That hardly seems fair,' he said. 'Why won't they let you enter the contest? And ... um .... who's "they"?'

Arthur got to his feet and began walking again, ranting all the while. 'Those **dimwits** who run the competition,' he replied. 'They've raised the entry fee from one shilling to two shillings! It's bordering on corruption! And it's not like Lord Farthington needs the money – he already owns a castle. They're just scared that I'll win on Bacon!'

'Well, bacon is the breakfast of champions,' Drew said. 'In fact, I could do with some right now.'

'What?!' roared Arthur. 'THIS is Bacon,' he added, pointing to his pig, 'and I intend to ride him in the competition. But the organisers are clearly scared that Bacon and I are going to show them up,' he vented, his cheeks turning a frightening shade of pink above his beard.

'They're PETRIFIED of losing to a pig, so they want to make jousting a horse-only sport.'

'Well, I mean, that sounds fair at least ... doesn't it?' replied Frankie, thinking it sounded pretty **bonkers** to enter a pig into a jousting contest.

'Fair? *Fair?* You think it's fair?' Arthur shouted, his voice breaking a little. 'It's as fair as a bald patch in a lion's mane!'

'Why don't you just ride a horse, though?' asked Drew curiously.

'Because I don't *own* a horse,' Arthur roared, throwing his helmet to the ground in disgust. 'Besides, Bacon is not just any pig,' he declared proudly. 'He's the best pig in the county, and he's my **best friend**. And I'll ride him into that jousting contest if it's the last thing I do!'

CHAPTER 6

BACON THE PIG

In between shouting and fuming, Arthur announced that he was going home. He picked up his now-dented helmet and led the boys (and the pig) to a small cottage at the foot of a mountain.

'Hopefully we can find the Chalice of Flames tonight and be on our way home,' Frankie whispered as Arthur opened the door and they all went inside. 'I really want to show it to Grandad.' He felt a pang of wanting to see his grandad again, and hoped the old man was all right.

'Do you think it's OK to steal a chalice from the Middle Ages?' Drew asked. 'I mean, won't that stuff up the timeline of history?'

Frankie frowned. Then he said thoughtfully, 'The chalice goes missing at the jousting contest, so we won't really be *stealing* it, just saving it before it's lost. Right?'

'Right.' Drew nodded shrewdly. 'I'll keep my eyes peeled!'

Bacon appeared to have an open invitation to Arthur's house and, after happily collapsing in a corner, was snoring within seconds.

'Little do they know the pig is one of the smartest animals in the world, in fact they are probably smarter than us,' Arthur roared. The fact that Bacon had hustled himself into plum position on a woven rug suggested he was right. 'Horses this and horses that, I'm sick of everybody thinking horses are the Christmas holidays and eggs at Easter all wrapped up in one!' he bellowed as he threw some dry sticks into his fireplace.

Frankie's eyes darted around, taking in the cottage. Where did one hide a valuable **Chalice of Flames**?

'Do you actually know HOW to ride a horse?' Drew wondered aloud, without thinking.

For the first time since they'd met, Arthur was speechless. He turned and took a step towards the two boys, looking as if he were only now beginning to wonder who these pesky kids were. 'Who are YE?' he said with a furrowed brow.

'Er,' said Drew, looking to Frankie for back-up.

'Oh, I'm Frankie. Frankie Fish,' Frankie said proudly. 'I'm your great-great – er, I mean, I'm your nephew,' he said, nearly giving the game away before recovering quickly. 'I've come a long way to see you. All the way from ... Scotland.'

'Which one of my clan do you belong to?' Arthur asked, looking flummoxed.

Frankie knew that Arthur was one of twelve kids in his family and had become somewhat of a hermit who hadn't seen them in years – so he figured he should be able to fudge the connection.

'I am George's boy,' Frankie guessed, hoping he was swinging on the correct branch of the family tree. 'George and ... Elizabeth?'

Arthur looked confused. 'I thought Brian married Elizabeth.'

Frankie swallowed. 'Did I say Elizabeth? I meant Susan!' he said hopefully.

'Susan married Greg!' Arthur exclaimed, his brow crinkling.

'What about ... Lisa?!'

Arthur relaxed. 'Oh, *Lisa*. Sure, OK.'

Frankie dutifully ignored Drew's raised eyebrows as his best friend mouthed, '*Like Lisa Chadwick???*' with a sly grin.

'Yes, I'm sorry,' Frankie said quickly. 'It's been

a long trip and I usually call her Mum, not, er ... Lisa. And this is my friend, Drew Bird,' he added politely.

Arthur was losing interest in the conversation anyway. 'Does this mean I have to feed you?'

'I mean, it has been a long trip,' Frankie said, his tummy grumbling right on cue. A warm, beefy English stew sounded pretty good to him right about now.

'I'm so hungry I could eat the feet off a low-flying duck!' Drew announced. 'Or, you know

... whatever kind of meat a retired butcher has around the place,' he added hastily, in case Arthur got the wrong idea.

'Maybe after we eat, we can help you think of a way to find the money to enter the **jousting contest**,' Frankie said, which appeared to pique his uncle's interest. *And find that chalice before it gets lost*, he added silently.

'I guess it won't be the worst thing to have some company. I love Bacon but he really isn't much of a conversationalist,' Arthur said as Bacon's snore got louder, in either protest or agreement – it was hard to tell.

Uncle Arthur's house was made up of two rooms. One was a small bedroom and the other was the room Frankie and Drew were in, which had a bath, a trough for dishes and a fireplace, plus a makeshift table and chairs in the middle (and a sleeping pig). His possessions were piled unevenly in the corners.

Despite his early rumblings, Arthur proved to be a decent host. He got the fire going and even cleaned some dishes and cutlery for the first time in ages. Frankie generously offered to set the table as his uncle stirred a large pot over the fire. Drew couldn't yet smell exactly which meat he was cooking, but was hoping for either lamb or chicken (and definitely not duck feet).

'Here you go, boys, it's Uncle Arthur's Famous Pottage,' Arthur declared with the fervour of a *MasterChef* contestant, plopping the bowls down on the table.

'We love porridge,' replied Drew politely, picking up a spoon.

'Not porridge, lad, *pottage*,' Arthur looked at the blank young faces in front of him. 'Don't tell me you've never had pottage?'

Drew brightened. 'Thank goodness, I was hoping for a good meaty stew!'

'Meat? Meat in pottage? Oh, you're a riot,' Arthur laughed. 'Pottage contains beans, onions and peas. Dig in,' he added, as proud as the first bird who built the first nest.

The boys' faces contorted like deflated balloons. 'But Uncle, you're a *butcher* –' Frankie started, before Arthur cut him off.

'I know, I know. I'm a butcher who doesn't

eat meat,' Arthur chuckled. 'And that's why I retired. After all, a butcher who doesn't eat meat is like a dog who doesn't like to pee on trees!'

Frankie glanced into his bowl, his stomach rumbling with disappointment.

'It's just typical that a relative of mine is the world's first vegetarian butcher,' Frankie whispered to Drew, who was circling the grey, lumpy stew with his spoon. It looked like something you'd feed to a pig if you had nothing else left to feed it – yet Bacon was feasting on bread and carrots.

Arthur carried on in the background, 'Besides, I want to spend more time at home. A man's home is his castle, don't you know!'

The boys knew it would be rude not to eat, and besides, they didn't really hate vegetables. They both loved corn chips after all. They each put a spoonful of stew in their mouths, and immediately wished they hadn't. As he tried to swallow the vile mouthful, Frankie hoped two things: that his uncle's jousting skills were at least marginally better than his cooking skills, and that the chalice was worth the **torture** his tastebuds were going through.

CHAPTER 7

A CHALICE WITH NO FLAMES

Partway through dinner, if it could be called that, Arthur looked up, alarmed. 'You've nothing to drink – where have I left my manners?' he said.

'In the same place you left your cooking skills?' Drew whispered, and Frankie giggled.

'I've got homemade ale or cider,' Arthur continued, 'and I dare say they're almost as good as my pottage!'

'Um ... no, thanks,' said Frankie, trying not to choke. 'We're not thirsty.'

Arthur shrugged. 'Suit yourself,' he said. He rummaged around in a pile of hessian sacks and retrieved a pewter cup with two large handles, which he filled with cider from a wooden keg.

Frankie's and Drew's eyes grew wide as they kicked each other under the table.

'That's a nice cup,' said Frankie, trying to sound casual and not like his uncle had presented the grandest, most admirable-looking cup in history.

'Oh, this is no cup, young man. This is a **CHALICE**,' Arthur boasted proudly, 'and it's no ordinary chalice, I can guarantee that.'

'What makes it so not ordinary?' asked Drew, getting excited.

Arthur scratched his beard like he was considering whether to tell the boys a tale. Soon enough, a smirk could be seen through his facial bush. 'Tell me, lads, do you believe in **legends**?'

Over the next hour Arthur poured and re-poured cider into his chalice as he told Frankie and Drew the legend of the Chalice of Flames. He told them how he'd bought it from a witch who'd said that when the chalice caught fire all by itself it would reveal to him the path to becoming **King of England**.

'I used to keep it in a special box and check on it ten times a day, just waiting for it to go up in flames. But nothing happened. Then I thought I may as well get some use out of it, so it became my cider chalice.'

'So it's never caught on fire?' asked Frankie.

'Do I look like the King of England to you?' replied Arthur, cider dripping from his beard onto his paunchy belly.

'I guess not,' the boys conceded.

'Anyway, I've just decided this will be my final cider from this chalice,' Arthur declared.

Frankie's ears pricked up, and Drew's eyes widened hopefully. Maybe Arthur was going to give them the chalice and they wouldn't have to steal – er, rescue – it after all.

'I'm selling the chalice to pay for my entry fee to the jousting contest,' Arthur declared. 'I've given up on it ever working – that old witch must have seen me coming, and she's probably still **cackling** about the fool she sold it to. At least it holds cider well,' he said, before guzzling some more. Then he belched loudly and excused himself to use the outside lavatory. 'The thing is, boys,' he added on the way out, 'I'm tired of Lord Farthington taking the mickey out of me all the time. I want to show him that I'm made of sterner stuff – much sterner stuff than he can even imagine.'

As he shut the door, Frankie and Drew huddled together like a two-person football team trying to work out their next play.

'Let's take it and go,' Drew whisper-screamed before clutching the now-empty chalice.

'No!' said Frankie, snatching it from his

hands. 'We can't steal his chalice now. You heard him, he needs it to win the jousting contest. Otherwise he'll be the laughing-stock of the village forever!'

Drew groaned. 'But he said he doesn't even want it anymore,' he pointed out. 'Couldn't we just borrow it and then return it after your Show and Tell?'

Frankie shook his head sadly. 'This is supposed to be our last time-travel trip. Grandad's going to destroy the suitcase when we get back. And if we take the chalice, we'll ruin everything for Arthur – and maybe even for my whole family. We can't do that!'

'Can't we just give him money?' Drew suggested desperately.

Frankie huffed, but checked his pockets for any spare change. 'I don't think three Australian dollars is going to work, somehow!' he said.

Drew's shoulders slumped in defeat. 'What's your bright idea, then?'

'We just have to help him **win** the jousting contest and get his chalice back, and then convince him to give the chalice to us,' Frankie blustered, hoping this **ridiculous plan** he'd invented out of thin air might work. 'Besides, don't YOU want to see a man ride a pig in a jousting contest?'

Drew threw up his hands and conceded. 'Of course I do!'

There were a few reasons Frankie Fish barely slept that night.

First, Uncle Arthur only had one bed and he wasn't about to give it up for his guests, so Frankie and Drew had to sleep on the hard floor. Frankie felt like his back had been stomped on by a baby elephant. Second, he had never slept in a room with a pig before and this pig really knew how to snore. At one point in the dead of night, Frankie suspected that Bacon was doing it deliberately.

Finally – and this perhaps was the real cause of Frankie's tossing and turning – he couldn't stop thinking about Grandad. Was coming to England for a chalice really all that important, when the trip was at the expense of spending time with the old man? Especially if they weren't able to get the chalice anyway?

Just because Frankie couldn't imagine life without him didn't mean Grandad wasn't going to pass on one day. They had to make the most of the time they had left. And the first thing Frankie was going to do when he got back was give his Grandad a hug.

At least things between him and Drew seemed normal again, Frankie thought – and it was this comforting thought that finally sent him to sleep.

Drew, of course, slept without a problem, and nudged Frankie awake in the morning, exclaiming, 'Hey Frankie, you need to see this!'

Frankie's eyes felt like they were glued shut, but he managed to prise them open as Drew exited the hut with great excitement. 'Quick, Frankie, it's **hilarious**!'

Frankie wearily got to his feet and yawned all the way to the door. The cold air hit him in the face like he'd been slapped with a frozen fish. Drew was pointing to a fenced area beside the cottage.

He could hear Arthur mumbling and moaning, 'come on' and 'not that way, this way!'

Frankie turned to see his uncle in full knight armour - which seemed even more snug-fitting than it had yesterday - riding Bacon the pig. Arthur had a jousting stick tucked under his right arm; the grille on his helmet was open, and he was trying to look dignified. But Bacon wasn't sticking to the plan, as jousting needs the horse - or, in this case, pig - to run in a straight line at the oncoming knight and horse - or pig.

Bacon oinked loudly as he turned left, then right. He danced around in circles before crashing through the fence.

He didn't seem angry – in fact, Frankie detected a cheeky piggy smile.

'Your uncle is **absolutely bonkers**!' Drew laughed.

As the fence fell down, Arthur took the opportunity to jump off.

'Are you sure you want to ride a pig in the jousting contest?' Frankie asked, concerned that his uncle was about to become a laughing-stock with or without their help.

'It's just pre-contest nerves, lad. Bacon will be right as rain when the time comes,' Arthur boomed, trying to sound confident. 'Now, we'd best get going. It's an hour-long walk, and we do not want to be late and give Lord *Fartington* the chance to deny us our shot at glory.'

Arthur put the freshly washed Chalice of Flames into a hessian sack and tied it to his jousting stick, then popped the stick over his shoulder. Frankie kept a close eye on the sack as he picked up his own bag – or, rather, his suitcase. Arthur put Bacon's leash on, explaining he wouldn't ride him to the jousting arena because that would only tire him out before the competition, and they set off.

'So … why ARE you riding a pig in a jousting contest?' Drew asked, still puzzled by Arthur's strange choice.

'Simple,' Arthur snorted. 'When you go into **battle**, who do you want alongside you?'

'Not a pig?' Drew whispered to Frankie.

'Your best friend,' replied Arthur, 'and Bacon has been my best friend ever since I bought him at the market. Why do you think I became a vegetarian?'

'Oh, so you're not bonkers, you're just sentimental,' Frankie thought out loud.

Arthur considered this. 'A little of both, I would suggest.'

CHAPTER 8

A BAD DEAL

The closer they got to the jousting arena, the more they sensed a genuine excitement in the air. It was like walking to the stadium before a big football game, except that occasionally knights would gallop by on their noble steeds. People admired them as they passed.

A line of stables flanked the outside of the arena; several carriages were parked there, too. Inside, sawn-down tree trunks provided ample seating. Flags flapped in the wind, bonfires kept the crowd warm, and local farmers offered deals for their hot nuts, pork knuckles and rabbit broth.

Arthur marched straight over to the registration table, trying to look as regal as a portly man covered in metal walking a pig can possibly look. 'I would like to enter the jousting contest,' he bellowed loudly.

The lady at the desk had a direct manner. 'Two shillings,' she barked.

'I do not have two shillings, m'lady, as I was **mugged** on the way here,' Arthur said, lying through the grille in his helmet.

'Who mugs a knight?' replied the lady, who looked like she had just sucked a lemon. 'They must have been rather audacious.'

'In fact, m'lady, I was mugged by a gang of twenty knights,' Arthur blustered, while Frankie groaned quietly, 'and so I offer this in place of my entrance fee ...' He undid his hessian sack and pulled out the chalice. 'The famed **Chalice of Flames**!'

'Never heard of it and that's not worth two shillings,' the lady replied, her face as serious as a heart attack.

'You have not heard of the Chalice of Flames?' Arthur scoffed. 'This very chalice will one day lead its owner to the throne of England!'

There was a small moment of silence before **thunderous laughter** erupted from everyone in earshot. Frankie had never seen a pig blush before, but he was pretty sure Bacon's face turned pinker. Arthur quickly put the chalice away.

'Who spills such nonsense?' said a man in shining armour complete with a chain-link tunic and black robes. Everyone in the crowd turned to look at him. His belt housed a large and rather dramatic buckle of a skull, which appeared to be on fire. His chestplate was adorned with a dragon, which was definitely breathing fire.

'Whoever this guy is, he certainly likes fire,' Frankie whispered to Drew.

'He likes fire the way Miss Merryweather likes extracurricular activities,' Drew replied.

People in the crowd made way for the man in armour as he strolled confidently towards the registration table with a look so smug he could have won first, second and third place at the Annual Smug Awards, which of course he would have also hosted.

He had a thick mane of blond hair and, as was common, a beard, but whereas Arthur's beard looked like hair was trying to frantically escape from his mouth, this man's facial hair was trim and neat. His jawline was so sharp you could slice eggs on it. If they had TV commercials in medieval England, he would be selling swords, carts and offal, accompanied by cheesy grins and a hint of eye make-up. To complete the look, a small crown sat atop his luscious locks.

'Is he the king?' asked Drew, which drew a laugh from the walking sword commercial.

'Bahahaha,' he bellowed before tousling Drew's hair, 'looks like I have a fan.'

'He surely is not the king,' Arthur mumbled, removing his helmet so he could wipe his brow. 'He WISHES he were the king.'

'So says the butcher who cannot eat what he sells,' came the quick reply from the shining knight. He spoke in such a posh and honeyed voice it made the Queen sound like a cockatoo with a sore throat. The crowd roared with laughter, but to Frankie's ear it sounded a little forced. He even caught a local farmer nudging his son to laugh. 'Tell me, Arthur Fish,' the knight continued, 'are the rumours true?'

'No, they are certainly not true. I DO NOT bathe with Bacon,' Arthur protested, which caused more laughter from the audience – but it was genuine laughter this time.

'I had not, in fact, heard that particular rumour – which is disturbing on a number of levels if it is true,' replied the knight, who looked like he had just swallowed a rotten apple. He cleared his throat and composed himself. 'No, the rumour I was referring to was that you are going to ride a pig in the jousting contest. It sounds **utterly ridiculous** – but, then again, you are an utterly ridiculous human being.'

Despite this knight's impressive looks, Frankie was quickly discovering that he was rather mean-spirited. He didn't like the sound of people laughing at his uncle, no matter how distantly related they were. It reminded him, rather uncomfortably, of all the times people had laughed at *him*.

'It's not ridiculous,' yelled Frankie, coming to his uncle's defence. 'I've seen this pig in action and he is as quick as a fox, as strong as an ox and as smart as a … a …'

'Box!' Drew chimed in, trying to help.

'No, not box, boxes aren't smart.'

'I thought you wanted it to rhyme,' Drew apologised, before the lady at the registration table interrupted.

'M'lord, neither he nor his pig will be entering the contest, as he cannot afford the entry fee,' she declared with more than a smidgeon of joy.

'Oh,' the man who Frankie and Drew had assumed to be a knight but was actually a lord said, pretending the news had upset him. 'Too bad, so sad.'

'I may not have the entry fee in shillings,' announced Arthur, 'but I do have this – the Chalice of Flames!' He quickly whipped out the chalice again, to which the crowd responded with an underwhelming 'huh'.

'I was anticipating a bigger response,' Arthur mumbled in Frankie's direction.

'Oh, wonderful, you are offering a dirty mug as capital,' the lord spat, as if he had just been offered a mouldy potato for lunch (or, worse, a bowl of Arthur's pottage). 'I think we can do marginally better than that. Do you still own that ramshackle hut at the base of Devil's Mountain?'

'I certainly do. I love that hut,' Arthur boasted, 'and actually, I think of it as my **castle**.' He added curiously, 'Why do you ask?'

'Well, if you are so confident in you and your filthy animal's jousting prowess, then I shall allow you to put your beloved hut up as capital,' the lord pounced with a sneer.

'Don't do it, Arthur, it's not worth it!' Frankie begged, but he had already learnt that his uncle had more pride than smarts.

Before Frankie could say 'ham and cheese' – or Bacon could oink in protest – Arthur yelled, **'Deal!'**

CHAPTER 9

PiG VERSUS HORSE

Suddenly, Frankie was a lot less worried about getting the chalice than he was about his uncle and Bacon losing their home. To make matters worse, it turned out the lord was Lord Farthington, and he insisted on jousting against Arthur in the very first match of the contest – which meant Frankie and Drew didn't have time to come up with a plan.

'Uncle Arthur, do you really think you're, ah, ready to joust against Lord Farthington?' Frankie asked, concerned that his uncle was about to be not only **publicly humiliated**, but also severely injured.

'I don't have a choice in the matter, lad, but trust me, Bacon is primed for this,' Arthur said confidently as Bacon buried his head behind Arthur's legs.

Trumpets sounded as the crowd jostled for position. Lord Farthington took centre stage and began addressing everyone. 'Welcome, ladies and gentlemen, to the fourth annual Lord Farthington Jousting Contest.'

The crowd dutifully clapped and cheered. 'They love sucking up,' noted Drew. 'They're like a crowd full of Lisa Chadwicks.'

Frankie groaned. 'I couldn't imagine anything worse,' he replied.

'The first joust of the day will be none other than yours truly,' Lord Farthington spruiked as Drew made puking gestures. 'I shall be riding my noble steed, the magnificent **Sir Trottsalott**,' he announced and, right on cue, a horse that was every bit as magnificent as Lord Farthington himself appeared from the stables. Sir Trottsalott pranced around the jousting field, lapping up all the oohs and aahs from the crowd.

'He is just as in love with himself as his owner is,' whispered Drew. Sir Trottsalott's mane was black and bouncy, his tail was plaited, and he wore a cape-like covering that had a coat of arms on it depicting a lion fighting a dragon.

'My opponent is none other than our local, recently retired, non-meat-eating butcher, Arthur Fish, who will be riding ...' Lord Farthington paused for full and dramatic effect. '... A pig!' he said, laughing. This, of course, was the crowd's cue to begin **laughing uproariously** at Arthur and Bacon.

'Don't worry, Bacon, we'll show them!' Arthur said, trying to block out the jeers.

'Due to Mr Fish's measly financial situation, he has not been able to offer the very reasonable registration fee, so we shall instead be jousting for his rather paltry shanty at the base of Devil's Mountain.'

The more Lord Farthington spoke, the more Frankie could feel his **blood boil**. Lord Farthington had no need for Arthur's modest house – he was doing all this just for the sake of cruelty.

Lord Farthington gestured to one of several mean-faced, armoured men standing nearby – his henchmen – and one came over carrying a highly polished helmet. The trumpets blew once more as Lord Farthington put on his helmet, mounted Sir Trottsalott and galloped to one end of the jousting field.

'How does this work, exactly?' Drew asked Frankie.

Frankie thought back to the cartoons he'd seen when he was little. 'I'm pretty sure they make their animals charge at each other, and aim their jousting sticks at their opponent's chest in the hope of forcing them off their horse ... or pig.'

Drew's eyes widened. 'Sounds kind of violent. I can't imagine the Hedgehog teaching us that in PE!'

Arthur handed his hessian sack to Frankie. He put his helmet on and laid a piece of fabric decorated with the Fish family crest (well, it had a picture of a fish drawn on it) across Bacon's back. He gathered his jousting stick and said a little prayer to himself as he straddled Bacon, who appeared to be frowning. Frankie and Drew shot Arthur a hopeful thumbs up as Lord Farthington nodded to the trumpet player to begin proceedings.

Frankie could barely watch. Surely there was no way Arthur could beat Lord Farthington, who looked like he had just stepped out of a Disney film. But, if nothing else, Frankie's time-travelling adventures had taught him that strange things can happen. In fact, in Frankie's

time-warped world, strange things were more common than normal things.

Maybe a pig could out-joust a stallion.

Maybe Uncle Arthur was just bonkers enough to prove everyone wrong and win this thing.

Maybe Team Fish was in with a chance after all …

Without further ado, the trumpets blew: PRRRR-PRRR-PRR-PRRR-PRR-PRRRRRRR!

The two knights, such as they were, turned to each other from their respective positions. They were about forty metres apart with a wooden railing between them so that they couldn't crash into each other. And then they were off!

Sir Trottsalott gathered pace, his mighty chest heaving, his nostrils flaring impressively.

Bacon the pig, on the other hand, wobbled sluggishly towards his fate, oinking in protest the whole way as if screaming, 'This is a horrible idea!'

Arthur should have listened to Bacon – and to Frankie, for that matter – because a moment later Lord Farthington's jousting stick jabbed him hard in the chest, sending him flying off Bacon and into the thankfully thick mud.

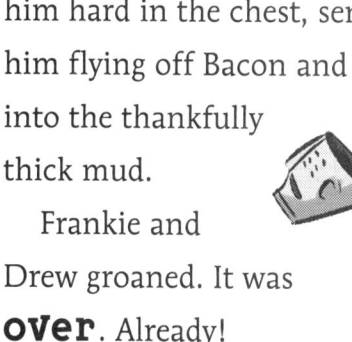

Frankie and Drew groaned. It was **over**. Already!

CHAPTER 10

A SPECTACULAR BACKFIRE

The crowd cheered as Lord Farthington and Sir Trottsalott did a lap of victory.

Clutching his uncle's hessian sack in one hand and the Sonic Suitcase in the other, Frankie ran over to Arthur, who hadn't moved.

'Is he dead?' Drew asked in horror. Frankie got on his knees. 'Uncle! Uncle! Are you OK?'

'I just lost my house,' Arthur moaned through the grille of his helmet.

'You certainly did, you fool!' Lord Farthington

lifted the grille of his own helmet so he could gloat at his poor opponent. 'I will take great delight in taking your ramshackle hut off your hands. With winter fast approaching, we could use more firewood to keep the castle toasty,' he announced with a grin.

That was the last straw, and it sent Frankie into an un-Frankie-like rage. 'You are NOT taking his house!' he shouted, leaping to his feet.

Members of the crowd ooh-ed and aah-ed as they shuffled around to look at him.

'And who are you, exactly?' Lord Farthington sniffed.

'I'm his nephew, Frankie Fish, and you are **not** taking his **house**!' he repeated, his fists clenched, his face red.

'I'm afraid a deal is a deal – unless you have something else you would like to offer up?'

Frankie took a deep breath. Even in his rage he knew he couldn't fight his way out of this. He needed to negotiate. 'OK ...' he said slowly, trying to buy himself more time to think.

What had worked for him and Drew in the past? What did they have to negotiate with? He was holding the chalice, but apparently it was worthless. The problem was, Frankie didn't really have anything else to offer. Except, of course ...

'How about this suitcase?'

To Drew's shock, Frankie held out the **Sonic Suitcase**. 'What are you doing?' Drew hissed.

'It's fine,' Frankie hissed back. 'We always get it back in the end.'

Lord Farthington's curiosity had been piqued. 'What is that, exactly?' he asked, leaning in.

Drew waited to see what brilliant lie his friend was about to unleash.

'This is the Sonic Suitcase!' Frankie Fish screamed at the top of his lungs. Drew Bird looked sicker than when he'd eaten Uncle Arthur's pottage – and it was about to get worse. 'And we are time travellers from the twenty-first century!'

'Um, what exactly are you doing, Frankie?' a completely flummoxed Drew Bird enquired.

'This is a time-travelling suitcase and it is worth far more than my uncle's cottage! And if you agree to give him back his house, I will show you what's inside.'

'Frankie! What are you doing?' Drew groaned.

'Don't worry, they think we're all *bonkers* anyway,' Frankie whispered back with a wink.

Lord Farthington jumped off Sir Trottsalott and made his way closer to Frankie. He put his hands out, and Frankie slowly handed over the Sonic Suitcase.

'Is what you say true?' Lord Farthington asked.

'Every word,' Frankie said honestly.

'Then if this is the case ... this is the work of **witches**, and thus this object must be burned!' he said. He looked Frankie in the eye before throwing the suitcase to one of his henchmen, then repeated his order. '**Burn it!**'

'Nooooo!' Frankie cried out before another

henchman detained him. 'The suitcase has nothing to do with witchcraft. The chalice does – a witch said it would one day **catch on fire** all by itself. Take that instead!'

'I'll take that as well,' said Lord Farthington, grabbing the hessian sack with the chalice in it, 'and it will most definitely catch on fire, for we'll burn it along with the suitcase!'

'OK, my friend must have been eating crazy beans for breakfast, it's just a regular suitcase,' Drew said, desperately trying to prevent their only way home from being destroyed.

Frankie, shocked that his plan had backfired so spectacularly, could barely speak.

'I could take the pig instead,' Lord Farthington said with glee. 'A big pig for the big feast tonight!' The hungry crowd cheered as Bacon cowered behind Arthur.

'NOBODY is taking my pig!' Frankie's uncle furiously declared. 'You can take my pride, but you'll **never** take my Bacon!'

'How about I give you my thumb?' Drew begged Lord Farthington. 'Look!' Drew then did that classic old party trick of making it look like his thumb had separated from his hand.

Lord Farthington was horrified, but when he worked out it was just a trick, he roared with laughter, prompting the crowd to do the same. Drew grinned cheekily; getting a laugh always felt good, and maybe – just maybe – his quick thinking could save the day.

'Do another one,' Frankie urged, staring desperately at their precious suitcase and hoping Drew's plan would work. Drew quickly tucked his hand under his armpit and started making **farting** noises, at which Lord Farthington guffawed, slapping his knee and wiping tears from his eyes.

'So, can we please have our suitcase back?' Drew asked the giggling lord hopefully.

Lord Farthington's cackle slowed to a titter. 'I'm sorry, but no. Burn it and the chalice, and the funny boy comes back with us,' he instructed his henchmen, before turning to Drew. 'You, my friend, are our new **court jester**!'

The crowd cheered as some of the henchmen bundled Drew into their waiting carriage, while another pair of henchmen carried the Sonic Suitcase and the chalice to a nearby bonfire.

Frankie stood, **frozen in horror**, as he realised the awful choice he was faced with: should he go after his best friend or the only thing that would ever get them back home?

In that moment, Frankie realised that by not choosing quickly enough, he'd made the wrong choice entirely – and that, in the end, it was too late for either of them.

As Drew shouted indignantly from the carriage, the henchmen slammed the doors shut and the horses began trotting away. In that same moment, the Sonic Suitcase was thrown onto the **bonfire** and went up in flames as though it had just been doused with petrol.

The disgusting smell of burning leather mingled with the smell of grease from the suitcase's internal mechanisms as the fire exploded with small sparks and inappropriately cheerful bangs.

The sight of Drew being led away AND his precious Sonic Suitcase being really and truly destroyed was all too much for Frankie, who felt the blood drain from his face as his legs went weak. As if from a great distance, he heard his uncle shouting furiously that his favourite cider cup had been burnt to a crisp.

And then, for the first time ever, Frankie Fish **fainted**.

And if he thought things couldn't get any worse, back home that's exactly what was happening.

CHAPTER 11

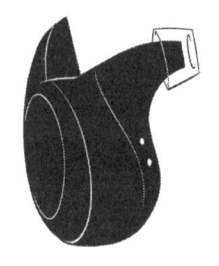

MEANWHILE, BACK HOME

Back in the Forbidden Shed, Frankie's sister, Saint Lou, was getting annoyed. 'Frankie! Can you hear me?' she kept saying into the mouthpiece she'd invented so she could keep in touch with Frankie when he went time-travelling. Usually it worked pretty well, but she was not getting any reply and the signal appeared to be dead. Then her eyes landed on the corresponding earpiece that Frankie was *supposed* to take with him on every trip.

The earpiece he'd clearly forgotten.

'This is not good,' she muttered, picking it up. 'But he'll still have the suitcase with him, so why isn't he answering my messages?'

She tried again despite knowing, somehow, that it was hopeless. 'Please, Frankie, if you can hear me, we need to get you home!' she begged.

There was a knock on the door. Lou quickly gathered herself, not wanting to worry anyone.

'Come in!' she said politely. The door opened; it was Nanna Fish, and she looked a little shaken.

'I think we may need to call the doctor, my dear,' Nanna said quietly. 'Your grandad is having a bit of a spell, and it's a pretty bad one. I've called your parents, too.'

Lou felt her heart pound like it was trying to break out of her chest. She really needed to get Frankie home quick. Time was running out!

CHAPTER 12

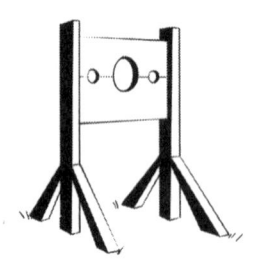

SUFFER IN YOUR STOCKS

The first thing Frankie noticed when he came to was that he was standing up. Standing up in a hunched-over position. Standing up, hunched over and with his hands and head stuck between two pieces of heavy wood.

This does not feel comfortable. Not comfortable at all, Frankie thought to himself as he tried to get his bearings. This was particularly difficult as he was a long way from home with his head wedged in some medieval device and he was looking down at his shoes. And then he remembered what had happened.

Uncle Arthur had lost his cottage and his chalice. *Grandad will never get to see the chalice now*, Frankie thought sadly. But then he had a worse thought: the Sonic Suitcase had been **destroyed**. Drew had been **kidnapped** to be a court jester. And neither he nor Frankie would ever get back to their own timeline.

Or see Grandad again, Frankie realised as his eyes filled with tears. *And I never even gave him a hug goodbye.*

He'd finally done it. On his final time-travel adventure he'd finally messed up his own life – not to mention the entire history of the world – so badly that there was no way at all to fix it. It all felt very ... final.

'Oh, look who's decided to wake up!' someone said nearby, and Frankie sniffed and did his best to look up. He could see he was in a room with stone walls, but that view was soon blocked out by a smirking, ruddy, wart-infested face that looked like it had run into many trees, many times. 'Welcome to Hotel Oddy. I'm your host, Oddy!' Oddy laughed right in Frankie's face; his breath smelt like a rotten cabbage that had been stored in rotten socks, and Frankie gagged.

'Where am I?' asked Frankie as he desperately tried to think of nicer-smelling things, like baked-bean farts. 'Is this a **dungeon**?'

'No, no – the dungeon is much worse than this. How many times do you need to be told, you're in Hotel Oddy!'

'But most hotels have more comfortable beds,' Frankie moaned.

'The exact point of difference that makes Hotel Oddy such a **fascinating** experience. Anyone can sleep in a bed, but to be locked up in stocks is much more enthralling, don't you agree?' Oddy hooted like a child who had just found his new favourite toy.

Frankie was eager not to anger his strange host,

so he politely agreed. His neck hurt, though, and he was suddenly full of unpleasant thoughts. He had seen stocks in movies and he knew they weren't good. 'How long do you think I will be your guest, if you don't mind me asking?'

'Well, that's not up to me, is it?' Oddy said, walking away. 'Lord Farthington decides who visits Hotel Oddy and who gets to leave in one piece,' he added. His laughter had changed to a much more **sinister cackle**.

Frankie felt his palms sweat and his heart beat faster as a truly awful thought leapt into his head and then out of his mouth. 'Are you going to **chop my head off**?!'

'Of course not,' Oddy replied sternly.

'Thank heavens,' Frankie mumbled, relieved.

'I'm just the host. Eddie the Executioner does the chopping,' Oddy added, 'and he doesn't arrive until morning.'

Frankie's chest heaved. 'But I'm just a kid – what did I even do? You can't chop off my head!

Nobody should be chopping anybody's heads off!' he cried.

'Nobody WANTS to have their head chopped off but, surprisingly, nobody complains after it's done,' Oddy said thoughtfully. 'In any case, Lord Farthington does not like witches or anyone who plays with witchcraft, so it comes as no surprise that he did not like your trickery with that suitcase of yours.'

'But it was JUST a trick!' Frankie screamed as he wriggled around in the stocks.

'Well, you need to make your tricks less witchy!' Oddy screeched back. 'Your friend's tricks were good fun. That's why HE gets to serve as Lord Farthington's court jester. The last court jester, Ronald, had lost his edge, so we had to let him go. Master Drew's timing was perfect – and in comedy, timing is everything.'

Frankie was glad to hear Drew was OK, but that didn't help his own situation. 'Maybe we could make a deal?' Frankie offered Oddy.

'Hmm, think you're the first to try to bargain your way out of this sticky situation? Are you trying to get me into **trouble**?' Frankie could feel Oddy's rancid breath on his cheek again as his host's voice became angrier. 'I don't like people who try to get me into trouble! It's not my fault you did a bad thing!' he screamed.

Frankie was worried he had driven Oddy down a dark path. 'Oddy, I'm sorry, I didn't mean to offend you,' he pleaded, trying to calm the odd man down. 'Oddy?'

There was no response. 'Oddy? I'm sorry. Please don't do anything silly.'

Not only was Oddy not talking, but Frankie could no longer smell his foul breath. 'Oddy?'

Oddy had clearly gone. But Frankie suddenly realised he was not alone.

There was a shuffling nearby, and a new but not unfamiliar voice whispered, 'Stay calm!' before throwing a bag over Frankie's head.

'What the – are you serious?' Frankie shouted

as everything went black. Then the weight on his neck eased as the stocks were lifted. 'Oddy, what's going on? Or are you the executioner?' he added, feeling panicked.

'No, I'm a friend,' came the voice. 'And I'm trying to help you, so **stop wriggling**!'

'Are you ... Uncle Arthur?' Frankie guessed, trying to keep the wobble out of his voice. 'And is the hood really necessary?!'

'It is, I'm sorry. You're coming with me and I don't want anyone seeing you until we're free and clear of this *lovely* hotel.'

And with that, the person hoisted Frankie up over his shoulder and carried him for several minutes, occasionally knocking his head on the low beams above ('Ouch!') or scraping his hands on the stone walls ('Be careful!'). Finally, Frankie felt a breeze on his arms, and knew they were outside. Then he felt the person toss him upwards with a grunt, and he landed on what was unmistakably the back of a massive horse.

'Hold on,' came that vaguely familiar voice, and before Frankie knew it, he'd been tied awkwardly to the saddle and the horse was galloping away from Hotel Oddy.

They rode for what felt like an hour, Frankie bouncing around on the horse like a ball in a tumble dryer. He occasionally shouted a question, like 'Who are you?' and 'Please can you take this hood off now?' but he never received a reply. He was glad to have his head out of the stocks, but he had no idea who this person was. Could he really trust that they were a friend?

He felt the horse slow and eventually pull up. The unidentified rescuer dismounted before helping Frankie to the ground and gently removing the sack from his face.

The sun had set, but there was still just enough light for Frankie to see the person in front of him. Well, he could see that they were covered in knight's armour.

'Sorry about the hood,' the young man said. 'We don't have much time. I managed to **sneak up** on Oddy and subdue him with some sleeping gas, but he'll wake up pretty soon. Anyway, are you OK?'

The knight was quite tall and fit, which meant it wasn't Uncle Arthur. So who was this strangely familiar person? Another unknown family member? 'What do you want with me?' Frankie asked nervously.

The knight shrugged. 'It's obvious, isn't it? I'm here to help you get home.'

Frankie felt tears spring into his eyes. 'There's just one problem,' he said, trying to sound brave. 'I'm not exactly from around here.'

'I know,' said the knight, and he began to take off his helmet.

'Who *are* you?' Frankie asked curiously, unsure what kind of reply he was about to get. Who in the Middle Ages could possibly help him and Drew get home?

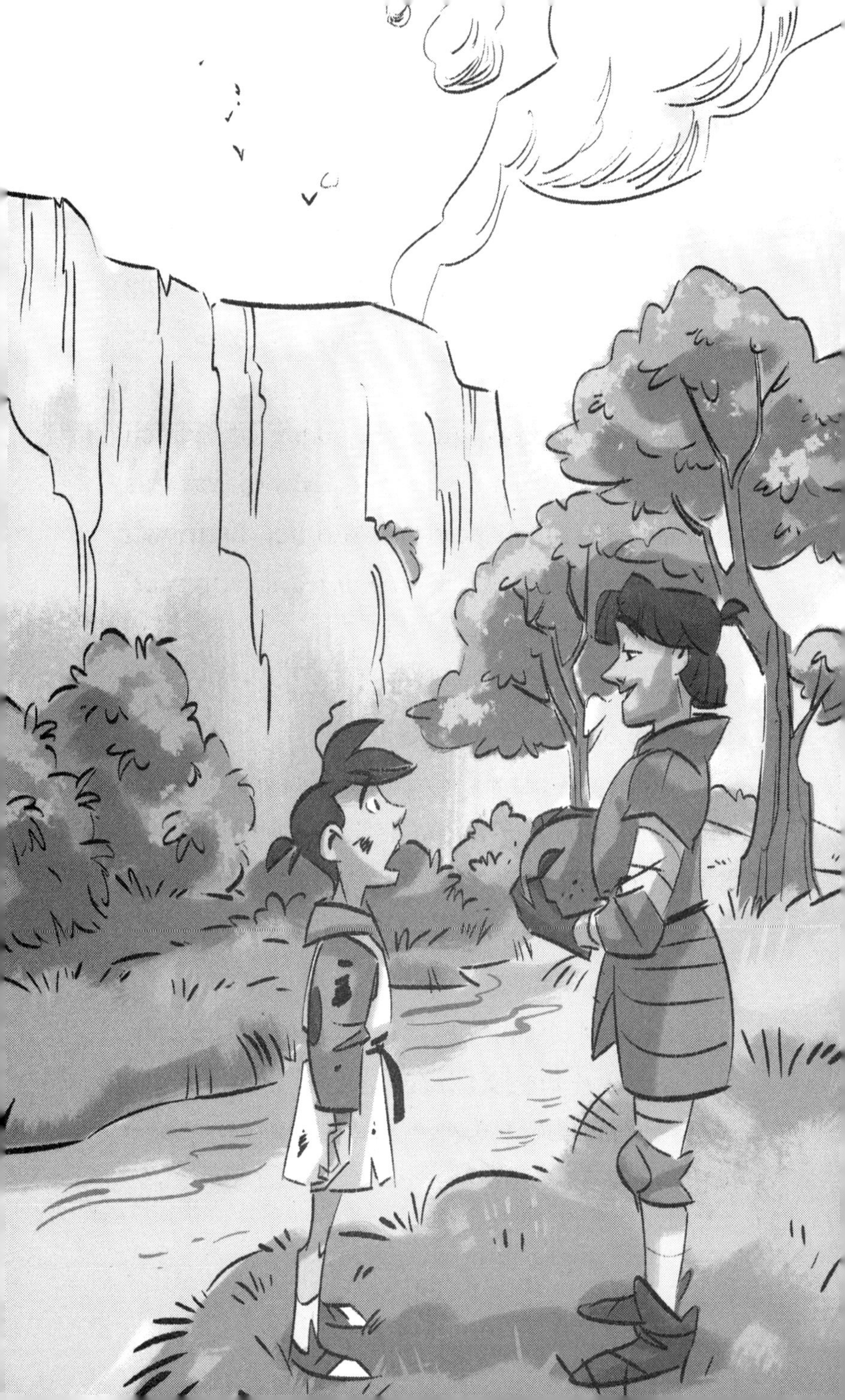

The knight's helmet was off now, and at first all Frankie could see was messy, shoulder-length brown hair, big brown eyes, and just the hint of a beard.

'You really don't recognise me?' the knight said, raising an eyebrow. 'I guess I'm a bit older now.'

Then he flashed a cheeky grin. 'I'm *you*, Frankie.'

CHAPTER 13

DREW BIRD LIVES AN UNDREAMABLE DREAM

Drew Bird was a born prankster. This was self-evident to anyone who'd ever raised him, taught him or befriended him: his dad, Gary Bird, was well aware of it, Miss Merryweather was exasperated by it, and of course Frankie Fish depended on it.

'If only Drew put as much effort into his studies as he does into practical jokes,' Miss Merryweather had repeatedly told Drew's helpless parents since his arrival at St Monica's Primary, 'he'd be a better student than Lisa Chadwick.'

Whenever Gary Bird asked his son what he'd like to do when he grew up, Drew offered a smorgasbord of far-fetched ideas.

'Professional YouTuber! Spitball sniper for hire. Water balloon connoisseur? Paper aeroplane pilot!'

It never occurred to young Drew Bird, as he pranked his way through life in the twenty-first century, that there was an impending job vacancy at Lord Farthington's castle in medieval England – but now, here he was. Through a series of unimaginable events, Drew Bird was now the centre of attention in the castle's Great Hall. He was drawing cheers and hollers from the packed crowd as Lord Farthington cackled and roared, sloshing his mug of mead over his dress shirt as he cheered the new jester on.

Drew had kicked off with a few sure-fire gags. 'What did one eye say to the other?' he bellowed with dramatic flair.

'What DID one eye say to the other?' demanded Lord Farthington.

'Between us, **something smells**!' declared Drew.

The crowd roared with laughter as Lord Farthington slapped his knee like he was playing Whack-A-Mole. 'His nose, his nose!'

'How do we know the ocean is our friend?' Drew asked the audience, which was quickly becoming putty in his hand.

'How? How?' they screamed.

Drew paused for effect before answering, 'It waves!'

Lord Farthington was laughing so hard, he was barely able to breathe. 'This kid's material is absolutely groundbreaking!'

'Why do bees have sticky hair?' Drew crowed.

'Why?'

'Because they use a honeycomb!'

'Stop it! Stop it!' Lord Farthington wheezed through his uproarious laughter.

Drew felt a delicious warmth rise in him as he looked around at the huge room full of adults who were not only listening to him, but loving him – just for being him. They were embracing all the things that adults in the twenty-first century had tried to discourage.

It's almost like they're rewarding my cheekiness, thought Drew, *instead of punishing it.*

Then he thought, *This is where I belong.*

And he hadn't even started on his armpit-farting routine yet.

CHAPTER 14

THE CAVE WITH THE MIRROR

Beneath the darkening sky, covered in horse hair and dust, Frankie Fish looked his older self in the eye. And then he fainted for the second time that day.

Thankfully, when he came to, his head and hands were *not* restrained in some cruel medieval contraption.

In fact, he woke to find himself lying down somewhere nice and warm, with a light flickering on the wall he faced. On closer inspection, once his sleepy eyes would allow it, he discovered that the wall was not a wall as such, but rather, jagged rocks. When he turned onto his back, he discovered the ceiling was also cluttered with spiky rocks, which pointed ominously downwards, like dragon's teeth.

As Frankie's senses began reappearing one by one, he could hear the pop and crackle of a campfire, and the scratchy feeling of a blanket that had been placed over him. The campfire gave off enough light for Frankie to see that he was alone in a cave but, just in case, he said into the ether: 'Hello, is anyone here?' There was no reply.

He sat up and tried to put the pieces together. He remembered the jousting contest and the awful Lord Farthington. He recalled Arthur's disastrous attempt to introduce pigs into competitive sport. He could still vividly see Lord Farthington's henchmen take Drew away, and the crick in his neck was testimony that he had definitely been detained in the stocks. Thankfully, Oddy's breath was no longer lingering in his nostrils, but that was where it all got very murky. One second Oddy was talking, the next he fell silent, and then Frankie had been spirited away on horseback.

But that was where Frankie's memory became as unreliable as a three-legged chair. He wondered if he'd been dreaming, because the next thing he could remember was a man telling Frankie he was him – which couldn't possibly be true.

'I probably hit my head when I fainted and have concussion,' Frankie told himself.

'Arthur!' he called out, hoping his uncle was around to provide some answers. No response. 'Bacon?' he whispered in desperation, wondering whether a pig could provide the keys to this foggy mystery.

Frankie got to his feet and moved closer to the fire.

'Throw another log on,' came the voice from Frankie's dream – but it wasn't a dream now. As Frankie looked at what appeared to be an older version of himself, still wearing knight's armour, it all came back to him and he did his best to ensure he didn't faint for a third time.

'**Wow!**' Frankie gasped, staring bug-eyed at his older self.

Future Frankie shrugged awkwardly. 'Sorry to scare you,' he said. 'I know it's strange and bizarre and, quite frankly, dangerous for two of us to be here –'

But Frankie was an ocean of emotion and couldn't deal with a complex time-travel conundrum just yet. He had more pressing questions.

'Is that ... *a beard?*' he asked in awe as he walked towards his older self. 'Do I grow a beard?!'

'Yes,' grinned Future Frankie. 'You successfully grow hair on your face, and lots of other places too, but I don't have time to take you on the full puberty tour. You need to focus because we have to get you home immediately!' he added firmly.

Frankie's eyes were still wide as saucers. Then he shook himself. 'Well, good luck with that – the Sonic Suitcase is as melted as cheese in a volcano,' he said gravely, and then realised that now probably *was* a good time to unpack the time-travel conundrum in front of him after all. 'Hang on ... if you're from the **future**, and the **suitcase** was **destroyed**, how did you get *here?*' He felt a surge rush through him, like electricity through power lines. He wanted to know the answers – ALL the answers – right now.

Future Frankie looked at him shrewdly. 'You know I can't tell you everything,' he said apologetically. 'In fact, I can barely tell you anything, but ...' Future Frankie paused, and let this hang in the air for a moment before revealing from under his coat a small, shiny blue suitcase.

Frankie didn't think his eyes could get any wider, but now they were as wide as family-sized pizzas. 'Is that ... the Sonic Suitcase?' he asked carefully.

'Oh no, that was burnt to a crisp,' Future Frankie replied, before adding, 'but it is a Sonic Suitcase. Lou and I have spent the past twelve years rebuilding it. OK, mostly it's been Lou. But I helped.'

'Lou?' Frankie felt his heart leap like an Olympic diver. 'Is Lou alive and OK? And Mum and Dad?'

'They're all fine.' Future Frankie smiled.

'And Grandad and Nanna Fish?' Frankie pressed. 'Are they alive too?'

Future Frankie's smile faded a little. 'Like I said, we really need to get you home, and we should go NOW. Lou and I did our best, but for some reason our suitcase doesn't exactly work like Grandad's original did. Our Sonic Suitcase 2.0 is a little **unreliable**. On top of that, things get pretty hairy around here tonight – there's going to be a big **raid** on Lord Farthington's castle.'

Future Frankie went to open the Sonic Suitcase, but Frankie stopped him. 'We can't go yet. Drew's in that castle and we need to save him.'

Future Frankie sighed, but looked like he'd expected this. 'I am not going to try to argue with you, or ah, me, I guess ... but I do need to tell you something.' His familiar face was deadly serious.

Frankie found a lump in his throat. 'What is it?'

'If we don't go home now, there's a danger that you won't see Grandad before ...' Future Frankie left this hanging in the air even longer than before. 'Before he dies.'

Frankie felt like he'd just had a cannonball fired into his chest. 'But ... he wouldn't. Grandad wouldn't do that to me. He would wait for me to get back.'

'It's not his fault,' Future Frankie said sadly. 'It's the Sonic Suitcase 2.0 – it's more erratic, more fickle, than the last one. I just can't promise you we'll be back in time.'

Frankie stared back in horror. 'But we don't have a choice!' he uttered. 'My best friend is trapped. We need to rescue him.'

Future Frankie nodded decisively. 'I knew you'd say that, obviously. So let's hurry. Want to see something cool?' He pressed a button on one of the suitcase's latches. Suddenly, the suitcase spun up into the air, then folded in on itself over and over again before landing on Future Frankie's wrist. Now it was a watch.

'That is pretty cool,' Frankie admitted. 'Was that Lou's idea?'

'I think we thought of it at roughly the same time,' Future Frankie answered sheepishly. 'Come on, we need to get going.'

So back on the horse they went and off to raid a castle before somebody beat them to it.

CHAPTER 15

THERE ARE NO CROCODILES IN ENGLAND

To Frankie's relief, he didn't need to have a sack over his head for this horse ride. They galloped back to Castle Farthington and for every stride the horse took, Frankie had a new question for his older self, who was more focused on the darkened road ahead.

'Do I finish high school?' he asked, pestering Future Frankie with questions that he knew his older self wasn't allowed to answer lest he stuff up Current Frankie's timeline (or, indeed, all of history). 'Do I finish top of the class?'

'Wow, if you think you could have been dux then you really do have a concussion!' Future Frankie snickered.

'Are Drew and I still friends?' Frankie pressed on. 'Hang on, is Drew still alive?' he added, panicking.

'Not if we don't **rescue** him soon,' Future Frankie said, rolling his eyes. 'Now shut up and let me ride!'

Frankie took that to mean that his friendship with Drew was *probably* secure for at least another ten or so years, so he respected his older self's request for peace.

The moon was full and bright, which wasn't ideal when approaching a castle to raid – a foggy night would have provided an ideal cloak of darkness. The Frankies pulled up at the edge of a forest, with only a grassy knoll between them and the castle.

As Future Frankie helped his younger self off the horse, he gave a slight grin at the madness of the moment. 'You know what this reminds me of?' he asked.

'Um ... that other time we came face to face?' younger Frankie replied cheekily. 'Like, twenty minutes ago?'

Future Frankie shook his head. 'Remember the three Grandads?' he asked.

Frankie's thoughts splashed in a puddle of fondness. 'Yeah! I remember. My first trip with the Sonic Suitcase in Scotland. Three Grandads were quite the handful – and that was before me and Grandad number one even liked each other!' He laughed, then felt his eyes filling with tears. He sniffled and wiped a tear away.

Future Frankie put a hand on his younger self's shoulder. 'It'll be OK, Frankie. I promise. Just try to keep it together till we get home.'

Frankie didn't know if his future self was just telling him this to calm him down, or if he knew something but wasn't prepared to share it. But in that moment, he knew he had to listen to himself. Well, to his **older self**. He took a breath and said, 'So what's our plan?'

'Well,' Future Frankie began, 'this may come as a shock, but before I saved you from the stocks I did some reconnaissance and drew this map.' He pulled some paper from his pocket and unfolded it; it was, indeed, a passable map of a castle drawn with a Sharpie.

'Are those **crocodiles**?' Frankie screamed, pointing at what looked like large lizards with pointy, inconsistent teeth swimming in a moat that ran around the castle.

'No, silly, there are no crocodiles in England,' Future Frankie reassured him. He paused. 'Those are **alligators**.'

'Great,' Frankie muttered. It was like being told there was not a snake under your pillow, there was a lethally venomous and very hungry lizard there instead. 'Do you at least know how many alligators there are?' he asked gingerly.

'Oh, I counted at least five, but who knows, really?'

Frankie could tell there was a drawbridge. There were also stick figures standing on each of the castle's viewing points. 'Those must be guards. But I'm guessing they're not actually made of sticks.'

'Sadly not. They are made of flesh and bone and have a large cache of weapons, including bows and arrows, swords, axes and giant vats of burning tar,' replied Future Frankie, sounding like a real Debbie Downer.

Frankie noticed the whole middle bit of the castle was blank on the map. 'And what about this bit – what's inside the castle? Please tell me you know what's inside!'

'Look,' Future Frankie said awkwardly. 'You know I'm not allowed to tell you anything about the future. But even if I could, the last time I did this was twelve years ago. I barely remember what happened! You just have to trust me that we'll get through it, OK?'

'Well, OK, but... how?' Frankie was beginning to fret; between the alligators and the vats of tar and the **not-having-a-single-clue** what was about to happen once they were inside the castle, this mission was looking pretty bleak. Could he even trust that Future Frankie remembered that it all turned out OK?

'Seriously, Frankie, relax!' insisted Future Frankie. 'I read up on this castle back home, and although there were no pictures or maps the website did say there were a ton of secret tunnels, chambers, cells, trapdoors and booby traps.'

Wow, future me really knows how to make something bad sound like something MUCH worse, Frankie thought.

On cue, Future Frankie added, 'Of course, that's on top of the impending raid. That really puts the pressure on us to move quickly.'

Yep, it looked like Frankie would NOT grow into a sugarcoat-it-with-a-cherry-on-top kind of guy.

Young Frankie Fish was about to throw his hands in the air and give up in the face of this almighty challenge. How could the two of them – the two of *him* – POSSIBLY charge their way into this **giant fortress** against a **trained army** ready to pour **burning tar** on their heads?

But then Frankie had an idea. And, just like all the other ideas he'd had throughout his adventures, it came at JUST the right time. But, just like all those other times, Frankie wasn't completely sure if it was a good idea ... or an absolute stinker.

'What else can you tell me about this raid?' he said thoughtfully.

'Well, I can say that it's led by a rival family,' said Future Frankie. 'The Brickendens, I think. I remember because I thought they sounded like a Lego family!'

Frankie forgot himself for a moment. 'What kind of Lego do you have in the future?'

'Stop it!' said Future Frankie. Then he glanced from side to side and whispered, 'But definitely don't open your Avatar 2 Lego set, it'll be worth a fortune one day!'

Frankie silently pumped his fist.

'Why did you ask about the Brickendens?' his older self asked.

'I'm just thinking we could come to the castle as friends, good Samaritans, to warn of the impending raid,' mused Frankie. 'So we wouldn't even have to sneak in. They might let us in the front door.'

'You know what?' said Future Frankie, scratching his chest thoughtfully. Then he grinned at his younger self. 'That is absolutely *not* the worst idea in the whole world.'

And Frankie grinned back, feeling a small glow of hope burn in his chest.

CHAPTER 16

NOT THE WORST IDEA IN THE WORLD ... OR IS IT?

As the Frankies rode their shared horse slowly towards the castle, completely unarmed, the younger one tried to think of conversation topics that didn't involve the older one spoiling the future.

'Does Uncle Arthur find somewhere new to live?'

'I can't tell you that, because technically that's part of the future.'

'Oh,' said Frankie, stumped. He thought for a while longer. 'Does this horse have a name?' he said eventually.

'Well, no, not yet,' replied his older self.

'What kind of monster doesn't give a horse a name?'

'I've only had the horse for a few hours,' said Future Frankie. 'I didn't bring it from home. Sorry to break the news, kiddo, but you're not riding a horse from the future!' He laughed before adding, 'Why don't you name it?'

Frankie barely had to think about it. 'Alfie is a good name,' he said quietly.

'Just so you know,' Future Frankie called over his shoulder, 'this horse is a girl.'

Frankie shrugged. 'Alfie works just fine for a girl, too.'

Suddenly, they heard two voices shouting from high up in the castle.

'Halt! Who goes there?'

'Identify yourselves!'

They'd arrived at last. Frankie crossed his fingers tightly, hoping his plan really would work and that they'd be on their way home before long. *Hang on, Grandad,* he thought.

Just as Future Frankie was about to speak, his younger self gave him a tap on the shoulder. 'May I?' Frankie asked politely.

'Sure.' The older Frankie shrugged.

Frankie Fish hopped off the newly named Alfie and landed in the deep mud below, muttering, 'Is there anywhere it's not muddy?'

Then he straightened up, cupped his hands around his mouth, and yelled: 'My name is **Francis Fish the Third**,' which wasn't actually correct, but he thought it sounded more medieval, 'and this is my travel companion...' He paused, not sure what to call him and reluctant to get into time-travel conundrums. 'This is my travel companion, **Sir Justin Bieber**,' he said finally, trying hard to prevent a giggle.

'How did you know the King knighted Sir

Bieber?' whispered a stunned Future Frankie.

'What do you want?' the guards echoed back.

'We come to you unarmed, but warning of danger ahead. There is a raid planned for this very castle on this very night. We ask you to warn Lord Farthington and allow us safety within your four walls.'

'Who seeks to raid Farthington Castle?' ricocheted a sole voice from the high right corner.

'The Brickendens, sir,' Future Frankie boomed back. 'They, er, stormed my castle too. They are a fierce enemy, however we felt that by forewarning you, you would be well placed to hold them off. All we ask is for you to lower your drawbridge and grant us safe harbour until the danger passes.'

'Which castle of yours did they storm?' a guard called suspiciously.

'Um ...' Future Frankie stammered, realising he had made the mistake of overindulging in a lie.

'Castle Grayskull,' younger Frankie quickly intervened, crossing his fingers behind his back.

Long moments of silence followed as our heroes awaited a response, hoping the guards weren't loading vats with burning tar. Finally, the eerie quiet was broken by the equally eerie sound of the drawbridge slowly lowering with an echoing, clanking sound.

'Pssst,' Future Frankie whispered, elbowing his younger self in the ribs. 'Put your fingers in your ears.'

'What for? The drawbridge isn't that loud,' a puzzled Frankie said.

'Trust me,' came the firm reply.

Frankie knew by the sound of his own voice when he was being deadly serious. He stuck his fingers in his ears.

THUD! The thump of the drawbridge hitting the ground was enough to wake a ghost. Two guards with impossibly large swords at their waists approached, and the taller, skinnier one spoke first. Frankie could just hear him. 'If this thing you say is not true, you will go to the gallows, understand?'

'It's totally true. What a weird thing to make up,' Frankie reiterated.

That was when the plumper one recognised Frankie. 'Hang on, aren't you the kid who escaped from the stocks?'

The skinnier one jumped like he'd been shocked, and in that moment both Frankies knew they'd been caught out. Younger Frankie felt a sinkhole opening in his chest – this was the most disastrous adventure he'd ever been on! And the stakes were sky-high this time. If they didn't find Drew, he'd be stuck here forever – or, even worse, they'd ALL be **stuck here forever**, and Frankie would never see Grandad again. And Frankie didn't even want to think about the disastrous effect of having two versions of the same person stuck in the same timeline – not only for the two people, namely himself and, well, himself, but for the space-time continuum. How would it even be possible? Would it change history forever?

Frankie could feel the panic rising now, rising in his chest, and he was just about to start screaming when ...

A loud screech pierced the air, like a train with an unbelievable sound system was about to collide with them. Instinctively, Frankie closed his eyes, kept his fingers in his ears, and bent over to avoid whatever was about to happen.

The screeching was over almost as quickly as it began, but Frankie waited a few seconds until he was sure he was still in one piece. He opened his eyes and lowered his hands to his sides before looking at the guards.

They looked stunned, as if they were **frozen in time**. Completely still, not moving a single muscle.

'Come on,' Future Frankie said, spitting out a whistle on a thin chain necklace and jumping

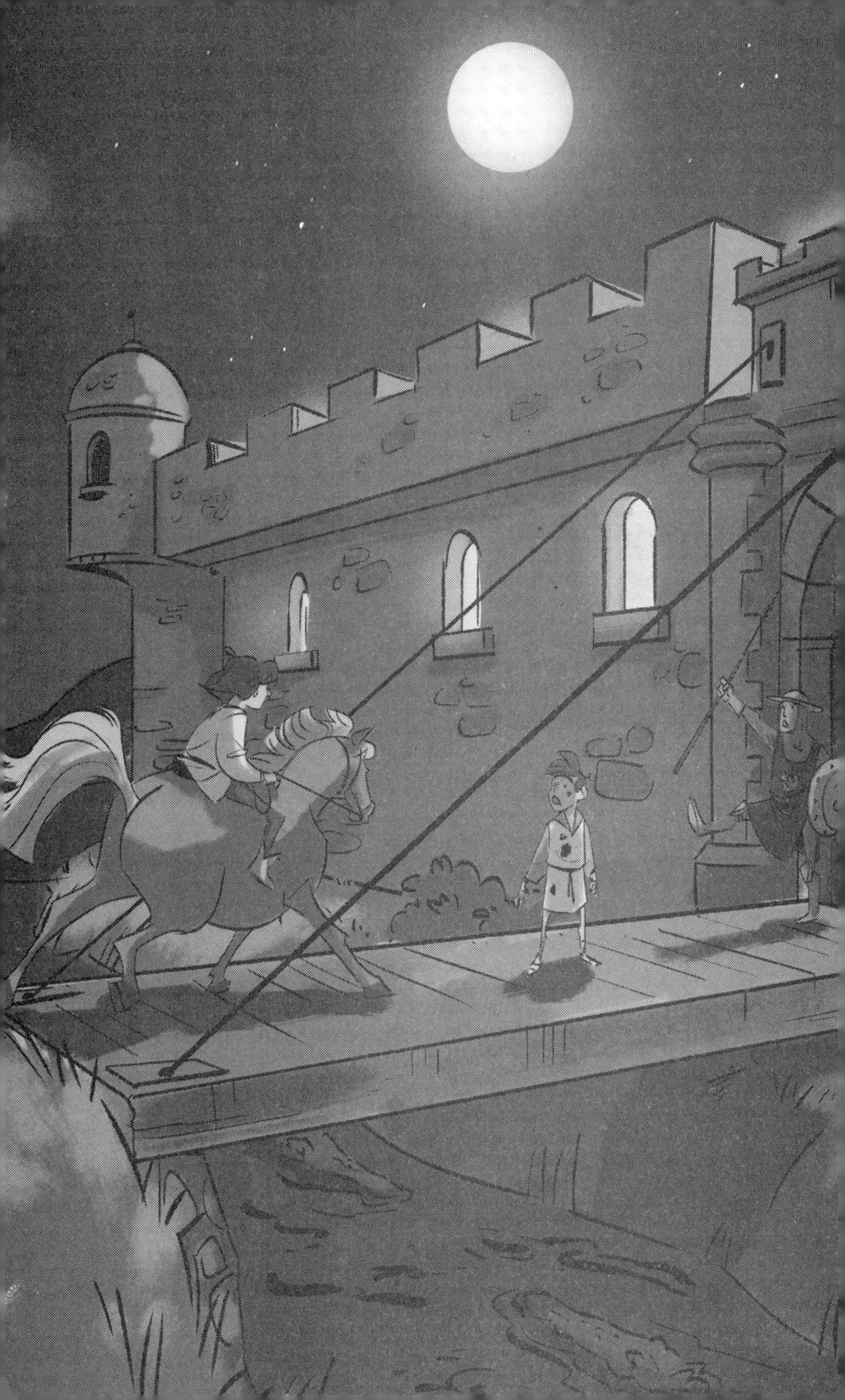

down from Alfie the Girl Horse. 'Don't act like a stunned toadfish! They'll be awake soon and you won't want to be standing there!'

'What just happened?' asked Frankie, trying to keep up both literally and metaphorically. 'What is that?'

'It's a new toy, one of Lou's inventions. A **Stun Whistle**. Doesn't work if you're blocking your ears,' he said. 'But the effect only lasts a minute or so, so we have to hurry!'

Alfie cantered obediently behind the two Frankies as they raced on foot across the drawbridge, decidedly ignoring the alligators swimming in the dark waters below.

On the other side of the drawbridge they emerged into a courtyard within the castle walls.

'Thankfully, the Stun Whistle doesn't exactly work perfectly,' Future Frankie added with a devilish grin, 'and it tends to erase your memory from the previous fifteen minutes. Quick, hide in here.'

He tied Alfie the Girl Horse to a post, then pulled Frankie behind a wide pillar just as the two bamboozled guards walked past. One muttered, 'What just happened?' and the other replied, 'Let's not talk about this EVER again.'

Future Frankie winked at his younger self before calmly walking out from behind the pillar and approaching the baffled guards. 'Excuse me, my good men, could you direct me to the court jester's quarters? I have a routine request from Lord Farthington himself.'

The tall guard – who looked like he may have had small cartoon birds swirling around his head – said dizzily, 'Take the first left once you're inside, then go right, head up the stairs and then it's the third bedroom on the left, you can't miss it.'

Frankie always hated when people said 'you can't miss it' because, in his experience, whenever somebody told him 'you can't miss it', he missed it. Luckily, two Frankies were better than one and they managed to follow the guard's directions and arrive at the door within minutes.

That was easy, both Frankies thought to themselves.

Lo and behold, when they knocked it was answered by none other than Drew Bird himself, medieval court jester.

'Frankie!' Drew screamed in delight before giving his best mate a hug tighter than skinny jeans on a hippo. 'I didn't think I'd ever see you again. What are you doing here?!'

'I'm taking you home, of course,' Frankie replied with a grin. 'And you won't believe who this guy is,' Frankie added, thumbing at his older self.

Drew looked both Frankies up and down. 'I think I can guess,' he said, 'though I never would have thought you'd grow a beard in the future!'

Frankie grinned. 'That's probably not the most surprising thing about this whole situation,' he said, 'but we can talk about that later. Right now, we've got to go!'

Suddenly, Drew's grin slid off his face. 'Oh, Frankie, there's a problem,' he said. 'I don't actually WANT to come home.'

CHAPTER 17

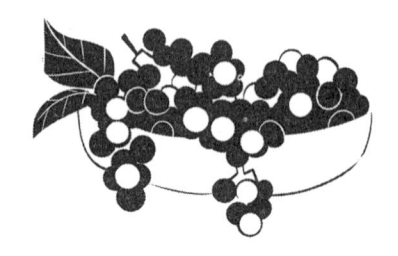

DREW BIRD:
RELUCTANT FLYER

Frankie could not believe his ears. '*What* did you just say?' he cried.

Drew Bird stood there, looking *very* apologetic and more than a little ridiculous in his coloured slacks, a puffy shirt and a jester hat complete with a bell on its tip. His bedroom was absolutely enormous, and in the centre was a huge four-poster bed with pillows as big as pigs. Bowls of grapes and goblets of water sat on a candle-lit table near a huge stained-glass window that overlooked the surrounding forest.

'I said,' Drew uttered, before taking a deep breath, 'I'm not coming home. I'm staying here.' He shuffled uncomfortably and the bell on his hat tinkled.

'Hang on,' Frankie gaped. 'This is a joke, isn't it? Of course it is. The ultimate prank from the ultimate court jester. Classic!'

Frankie held out his fist for a fist bump, but there wasn't one forthcoming. He looked more closely at his best friend and, in a heart-wrenching instant, Frankie recognised the look in Drew's eyes. Ninety-nine per cent of the time Drew had a cheeky sparkle in his eyes, a sassy flicker, a glimmer of **naughtiness** – but not now. Now he had a face that was as focused as a dog at dinnertime. Frankie had seen this look only recently, when Drew had requested permission to go back in time, alone, to explore his family's heritage. It was a look that meant only one thing: he was serious. Frankie had felt pretty hurt when Drew had wanted to time-travel without him, but this was even worse. Now, it seemed Drew wanted to live without Frankie and his friendship – **forever**.

'But why?' Frankie asked, his voice barely making it through the question.

'Last night I performed for the entire castle and I had them in stitches. I think this is what I want to do with my life,' Drew said earnestly. 'All this time I thought it was about pranking or bottle-flipping, but THIS is it. It's MEDIEVAL IMPROV THEATRE!'

'Why can't you perform at home? Miss Merryweather would love you to get involved with her theatre group! I hear she's planning a summer production of *The Greatest Showman*,' Frankie offered.

Suddenly, there was a lot of yelling outside. Drew and the Frankies rushed over to the window, nearly knocking the table of grapes to the floor.

Young Frankie couldn't quite make out what the kerfuffle was, but Future Frankie knew immediately. 'The Brickendens,' he groaned. 'We need to get out of here NOW!'

Frankie turned to Drew, his face white. 'OK, Drew, you've caught the improv bug at a REALLY inconvenient time, and I get that, but you need to come home with us!' he begged.

'You're not the boss of me,' Drew said sharply. 'I knew you wouldn't understand, but my mind is made up – and you need to go.'

Frankie couldn't comprehend what was going on. It was like somebody had thrown his life into a blender and pressed **turbo speed**. This was his one and only friend, the friend who'd come along at exactly the right time. The person who had saved him from the lonely hell of being friendless at school. Frankie was about to lose Grandad and now he was losing Drew. He felt like he had been **punched in the gut** by all three Mosley triplets at once.

He felt a surge in his stomach that made its way up through his chest, through his throat, and then it happened: Frankie Fish burst into tears in front of his very best friend. 'Please, Drew, please!' he begged again.

Drew couldn't speak, but he slowly shook his head.

Frankie looked at his future self. 'Did you know this was going to happen? Is this how it ends?'

It seemed Future Frankie had also caught the highly contagious can't-find-words virus, as he simply shook his head.

Drew took a goblet of water from the table and held it out, looking very sorry. 'Here,' he whispered. 'Take this. It will be perfect for Show and Tell.'

'No thanks,' Frankie replied, gathering himself. **'Good luck, Drew.'** He took a shaky breath, then nodded at Future Frankie.

Future Frankie said to his wrist, 'Suitcase engage!' On that command his watch leapt off his wrist and into the air, spinning and then unfolding into the Sonic Suitcase 2.0 before dropping right into his waiting hand.

'OK, that's cool,' admitted Drew.

'Take us home, *Suity!*' Future Frankie yelled as flaming arrows flew in both directions outside the window.

'Did you just call it Suity?' Frankie muttered.

'Yeah, it's kind of a thing now,' his older self

answered, sounding a little sheepish.

Everyone waited for a long moment, but nothing happened. They could hear roars and shots being fired outside.

'Um, how long does Suity take to start up?' Frankie asked out of the side of his mouth.

'It's supposed to be immediate,' Future Frankie said, confused. He glanced around the room for answers. 'Oh, I know the problem. These castle walls are too thick, I bet you they're blocking the signal.'

'Signal?' Frankie repeated, feeling like he was learning about time travel all over again.

'Suity runs off 12G from the future,' Future Frankie confirmed. 'We need to get outside quickly so we can access it!'

'Out there?' Frankie said in a squeaky voice, pointing at the fiery battle taking place. Then he had a better idea. 'How about the roof instead?'

'Nice thinking, kid,' Future Frankie replied, looking impressed.

'Are you SURE you don't want to come home?' Frankie asked Drew one more time.

'I'm the class clown who became a court jester. I *am* home, Frankie.' Drew smiled, looking as certain as mud on a farm. 'But I can show you the fastest way to the roof. Come on!'

Drew bounced out of the room with both Frankies close on his heels. Around them, the noise was getting louder and more violent both outside and inside the castle. Frankie was nearly knocked to the ground as a line of knights marched past them, the one in front barking orders at a group of other knights further ahead. Women gathered their kids and ushered them to safety – or at least, what they hoped was safety.

The trio ran through the long, stone hallways as knights around them loaded their bows with arrows. It was **pure mayhem** as the panic of being raided set in. Children could be heard crying, horses braying, chickens clucking for their lives.

And then, just as they rounded a corner, they came face-to-face with none other than Lord Farthington, who was in quite a state, and some of his henchmen.

'Jester!' he cried upon seeing Drew, completely ignoring the Frankies. 'I would like to stay and fight, but my henchmen here are insisting I go to the bunker to stay safe from impending danger. I'll need YOU to lighten my mood – so YOU'RE coming with me!'

CHAPTER 18

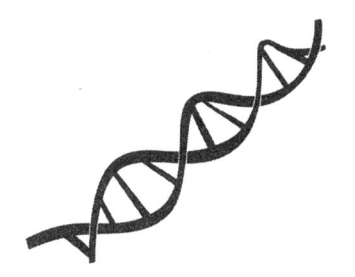

TO THE ROOFTOP!

Frankie never even got to say goodbye to his best friend.

'I'm sorry, Frankie!' Drew yelled as the henchmen bundled him away. 'Take the stairs!'

And then Drew was gone, and the two Frankies were on their own. The chaos of the moment meant Frankie wasn't processing the fact they were actually, finally, REALLY leaving Drew Bird in the Middle Ages. It's pretty hard to think straight when you're in a castle in the midst of a historical and violent raid.

As they turned to go up the stairs, the two Frankies were met with an unwelcome sight: Oddy coming down towards them.

Oddy recognised young Frankie straight away. 'Well, well, well,' he sneered, grabbing Frankie's shoulder, his mealy breath hitting Frankie in the face like a car airbag.

Frankie's mind ran to being put back in the stocks, but in a nanosecond he saw Future Frankie jam the Stun Whistle in his mouth and his fingers in his ears. Frankie had just enough time to stick his own fingers in his own ears before his older self blew on the Stun Whistle with all his might.

Unfortunately, at that exact moment, an explosion rocked a nearby room, drowning out the Stun Whistle's piercing shriek. In a flash, Oddy ripped the whistle from Future Frankie's mouth and tossed it to the ground.

'Nooooo!' shouted Future Frankie, looking crestfallen.

'Don't you know I hate whistles?' Oddy hissed, his breath as foul as ever. 'Guards, **arrest** these two criminals!' he hollered.

Frankie had just enough time to scoop up the Stun Whistle before he and his older self were overwhelmed by two nearby knights. 'Take them to the dungeon.' Oddy smirked evilly as the knights quickly tied the Frankies' hands behind their backs.

Frankie and Future Frankie stared at each other desperately. How on earth could they ever get enough signal from a *dungeon* to get back home?

Frankie Fish was no stranger to dark, dingy dungeons. He had experienced one back in Imperial China and now here he was in an eerily similar one in the Middle Ages in England. At least this time he had himself for company, so to speak.

'This really wasn't worth it,' he muttered. 'All this for a chalice with a made-up legend.'

'I guess you could say a lot of our adventures were like that. We went to Norway and nearly got beheaded by Vikings because we wanted to win a Halloween contest, and we went to Ancient Egypt and came very close to being **buried alive** in a tomb because we wanted to humiliate the Mosleys,' Future Frankie recounted.

'So, you're saying I have only myself to blame?'

'Yes and no. I guess what I'm really saying is, yes, we have gone on some **silly adventures** sometimes and, yes, they have been for silly reasons. And, yes, we have nearly died many, many times and, yes, we risked the future of humanity too many times to mention – but would you take any of it back? The time we spent with Drew, Lou, Grandad and Nanna – let alone the people we met on our travels, like Ping, Birger and Brynjar, even Alexis, as annoying as he was, and Salama. We hung out with Milly the Kid and met Laughing Sparrow in the Wild West. We have seen things nobody will ever get to see again. Would you give any of that back?'

Frankie thought about it. Here he was in a dark, dank cell, trapped in time. He was more than likely going to be taken to the gallows – but he couldn't get the memory of that first time-travelling trip to Scotland out of his head. Arriving in 1952 in a green field scattered with boulders. He could almost smell the wet grass and feel the cold air on his face. He could vividly recall the grey clouds that hung ominously overhead, and he smiled at the memory of finding Grandad snoring in the mud.

'Nope,' he said quietly. 'I wouldn't change a thing.'

Future Frankie checked Suity and confirmed there was even less of a signal than there had been in Drew's bedroom. They were out of plans, and out of ideas. Now they had to wait for a miracle.

'Future Frankie?'

'Yes?'

'Will I ever see Grandad again?'

Future Frankie didn't answer.

Meanwhile, the bell on Drew's hat rang time and time again as he, the court jester, danced a merry jig in front of Lord Farthington and two members of his entourage.

But Lord Farthington was no longer laughing or slapping his knees in appreciation of Drew's antics. Now, he just looked **baffled**. So Drew decided to change tack and go for a gag instead.

'Um,' Drew stammered before thinking of the perfect joke, 'how do billboards talk?'

'What's a billboard?' Lord Farthington whispered to his henchmen, who both shrugged.

'They use sign language!' Drew announced to piercing silence.

Drew could feel his mojo disappearing faster than a shadow on a cloudy day. 'What did one strand of DNA ask another strand of DNA?' he asked, a note of desperation creeping into his voice. 'Do my genes look OK?'

'Why aren't I finding this funny?' a flustered Lord Farthington roared.

'Perhaps because your castle is being raided and you're hiding in a bunker?' Drew unwisely offered.

The henchmen quickly jumped in. 'Are you suggesting the great Lord Farthington is **SCARED**?'

'Yes, is that what you are suggesting, Drew Bird?' Lord Farthington asked threateningly.

Drew immediately went into damage control. 'Oh no, of course not. Stories of your bravery are legendary, sir, but I also know how much you care about the state of your castle, as well as for the noble men and women who protect it,' Drew declared before offering a simpering little bow of the head. He couldn't help but think that the shine was wearing off his improv career.

'Yes, this is true,' Lord Farthington agreed. A tiny smirk appeared as his ego was stroked.

'You care so much, my lord!' agreed one henchman.

'Maybe too much, my lord,' said another, in a clear attempt to outdo his colleague in the suck-up stakes.

Then a third henchman, who'd just entered the bunker, attempted to outdo both of them. 'You absolutely do care too much, m'lord!'

he simpered. 'In fact, perhaps you should make an example of the boy who escaped the stocks. Oddy found him again on the stairs to the roof and threw him in the dungeon with his friend. That'll teach them to raid the castle with the Brickendens!'

Drew felt his tummy churn like he had just eaten ice-cream with orange juice and tomato sauce. *The Frankies!* he thought anxiously. Thinking quickly, he attempted to distract Lord Farthington with a robot dance.

'Check this out!' he shouted, but there was a problem: robots weren't invented yet, so it just looked peculiar.

'Well, that's not making me laugh, either,' scoffed Lord Farthington. 'It looks like your joints have stiffened.'

'Not funny at all,' a henchman unsurprisingly agreed.

'Do you have scurvy?' sniped another.

Starting to feel desperate, Drew began the chicken dance instead. But ...

'Why would you dance like a chicken when you know I hate chickens?' Lord Farthington roared.

Drew was feeling really **panicked** now. He felt like he couldn't do anything right for Lord Farthington anymore, and if things kept going like this he could be out of a job. In fact, he could be thrown in the dungeon with the others ...

I think I've made a huge mistake, Drew thought.

Hopefully there was still time to fix it.

'My lord, may I suggest the worry you have for your fellow people is causing you to, well, **freak out** a little,' Drew said, bowing very low. 'May I offer to take a small break, check on the progress of the raid and then report back to you with some good news? Perhaps then you'll see the lighter side to my hijinks.'

Lord Farthington nodded, looking very tired. 'Yes, you may be right. Off you go, jester. But return quickly!'

CHAPTER 19

A BIRD-BRAINED SCHEME

The cell was dark and cold, and Frankie was pretty sure he could hear rats scratching their way around the grubby chamber.

'So, what happens if we don't get out of here?' he asked his older self.

'I was trying not to think of that,' Future Frankie replied. 'But I guess if you, er ... *perish* here, it creates a true time-travel disaster because then I won't exist. So either I would disappear ... or it could be much worse.'

In the grim darkness, Frankie could just make out the worried look on his older self's (extremely handsome, it must be said) face. He let his answer float before replying with, 'Have you ever regretted asking a question as soon as you get the answer?'

Future Frankie gave a humourless laugh.

The silence that followed felt very loud, and Frankie was keen to distract himself from the scuffling of rats – and the prospect that those rats might eventually be their dinner if he and his older self didn't make it out of there.

'Hey, considering we might never get out of here, you've got to tell me something. What was the rest of my life like?' Frankie asked quietly with a cane toad in his throat.

'You know I can't tell you that,' came the reply from the darkness.

'Why not? If this is the end, and it seems like it is ...' Frankie swallowed, and then pressed on. 'What's wrong with giving me a little something?

Just to let me know what might have been in front of me.' He was trying to sound brave, but he could feel the tears on his cheeks racing to his neckline.

Future Frankie paused. 'I guess you're right,' he said eventually. 'OK, why not?'

Frankie sat up straight and wiped his tears away. 'Really? So ... what happens?'

'Well, I guess the biggest thing is that you won't believe who you marry!'

'Who?' Frankie begged. 'Someone super famous? Or even ...' He crossed his fingers tightly. 'Kimmy Klute?'

Future Frankie smirked. 'It's not Kimmy, but it's *definitely* someone from school –'

But before he could finish, the darkness was disrupted by a quivering light bouncing off a flame torch, and the clank of iron gates. Both Frankies rose gingerly to their feet, suddenly **frightened** of who might be coming for them. Was it Oddy or one of the henchmen coming to take them to the stocks – or even worse, was it the executioner, come to take them to the gallows?

As the light crept up the cell walls the Frankies braced themselves, and the older one put an arm tightly around the younger one's shoulders.

'Guess what I found!' came a familiar voice.

The tightness in Frankie's chest melted like an M&M in a furnace when the face that came around the corner was none other than the court jester's. Yep, it was Drew Bird, holding a large pair of keys.

'Drew!' the Frankies screamed at the same time.

'These were just hanging on a hook near the door,' Drew grinned, jangling the keys before unlocking the dungeon's gate. 'Let's go home, hey?'

The moment the gate was open, Frankie flung himself at Drew. 'What happened?' he said, squeezing him tighter than a bear in a bear-hug competition. 'I thought you wanted to stay! The class clown who became a court jester, remember?'

'I realised you're the person I love making laugh the most, Frankie Fish,' Drew said honestly, and **squeezed** him right back.

Frankie had never been happier. He and Drew were still best friends after all!

Future Frankie coughed behind them, but Frankie could practically hear his grin. 'I hate to break up the reunion,' his older self said, 'but we really need to get out of here.'

'Which way do we go, Drew?' Frankie asked quickly. 'I'm guessing we can't just walk out the front, or we'll have arrows in our chests sooner than you can say *heartburn*.'

'We'll figure it out. Let's just get moving!' Drew barked and began marching back the way he'd come.

As they sprinted up the narrow corridors, Future Frankie mused, 'Hey Drew, how did you know we were down here?'

Drew smirked. 'I was entertaining a clearly frightened Lord Farthington in his panic room when one of his henchmen mentioned you guys. It's hilarious – *Fart*ington is pretending that he wants to fight and defend the castle, but he's actually as scared as a scarecrow in a wind tunnel.'

Future Frankie halted immediately. 'So he's scared of the raid?'

'He sure is.'

Future Frankie smiled slyly. 'Let's go see him. I have an idea.'

Lord Farthington paced the bunker nervously. He almost jumped when there was a knock on the door, but was relieved to see it was his court jester, Drew Bird.

'Oh, jester, it's you. What's going on out there? It seems to be getting louder.'

Lord Farthington was correct – the mayhem was reaching fever pitch as the Brickendens were beginning to penetrate the castle walls.

'It is quite a situation out there, but I have somebody here who would like to speak with you,' Drew announced.

'Who on earth would you bring to my bunker? It better not be Oddy, his breath would stink this place up to the high heavens, and there are no windows!' the lord ranted.

'No, definitely not. This is Sir Justin Bieber.' Drew smirked, stepping aside to allow Future Frankie Fish to enter in full knight's armour.

'Who in the name of the king is Sir Justin Bieber?' the lord fumed.

'I am the leader of the army that is currently raiding your castle,' Sir Beebs announced.

'Bird, why have you brought my enemy to my hideout, er, I mean, special strategy and planning committee room?'

Sir Bieber stepped forward. 'I come in peace,' he declared, 'with the offer of a treaty. Agree to my terms and I will have my army retreat.'

'And what are your terms? If you think I am just going to hand over my castle you have another think coming.'

'No. We do not want your castle.'

'Then what is it you want?'

'We want you to let Arthur Fish remain in his house at the foot of Devil's Mountain,' Bieber stated.

There were a few moments of silence as Lord Farthington waited for further demands. 'Is that all?'

'Yes, sir, that is all,' Sir Justin said.

'Well, if it means surrender then of course

I was only taking it for a laugh and for some firewood,' he dribbled, 'so I agree to your terms.'

'I'll need it in writing.'

'Well then, I will write it up now, seal it with my famous wax seal and even send it to Mr Fish via my most trusted carrier pigeon, Squeaky.'

Drew and Sir Bieber waited for the contracts to be signed in Lord Farthington's fanciest quill, with **'P.S. No take-backs!!!!'** scrawled at the bottom. After it was sealed, the hairiest henchman was dispatched to deliver the contract directly to Squeaky.

Future Frankie shook Lord Farthington's hand and said, 'The moment we see Squeaky in the air, we'll call off our army. Pleasure doing business with you!' Then he turned to Drew. 'We'd best be off. Jester, can you show me out?'

Then he stepped out of the bunker with Drew, winking at Frankie (who'd been eavesdropping from outside), and locked the door behind him.

CHAPTER 20

THERE IS ALWAYS A FINAL HURDLE

The time-travelling trio raced down a darkened passageway, Drew leading, with only a flaming torch he pulled from a wall to help light their way.

'How do you know where we're going?' Frankie asked, doing his best to keep up.

'I don't,' Drew replied.

'What?!' said Frankie.

'Gotcha! Classic court jester joke,' Drew said with a laugh. 'Earlier today, one of the henchmen told me there's a secret escape hatch near a statue of the Farthington family crest. As soon as we find it, we're outta here.'

'How will we recognise the crest?' Frankie moaned.

'You've seen it before,' Future Frankie said. 'Try to remember!'

That was easier said than done while running through a medieval castle accompanied by the dull roar of **shouting** and **yelling** from outside, so Frankie decided to trust his back-brain to do the thinking for him and just concentrate on getting as far away from Lord Farthington as he could.

'Do you think Farthington will flip when he realises we weren't with the Brickendens and there is no retreat?' Frankie huffed as he ran.

'Technically we didn't do anything wrong, as we didn't change the outcome of the raid,' Future Frankie said, sprinting along. 'And sure, *Fartington* won't be thrilled, but we have his signature and he wrote *"No take-backs!!!"*, which I think is legally binding. As long as Bacon doesn't eat the contract – or Squeaky, for that matter – then his house should be safe.'

Frankie felt a small weight come off his shoulders. Deep down, he had been worried that it was his fault Arthur had lost his cottage. After all, he'd stood up for Arthur before the jousting battle – what if that had led the lord to make a bet on Arthur's house? History was such a tricky thing, and you never knew whether you'd made an enormous change or a tiny one, so it was better not to change anything at all. But now Frankie was sure that all had been put right with bonkers old Uncle Arthur, and he was proud of himself for defending him. As Frankie ran around a corner, he felt sorry that he hadn't had a chance to say a proper goodbye.

The two Frankies and Drew raced along more dimly lit passageways until they finally came to a long, wide corridor lined with statues. 'I hope it's one of these,' said Drew, breathing heavily as they stopped to examine them. 'There aren't many statues anywhere else in the castle.'

There were statues of all sorts of things – horses and people and birds and griffins and dogs – but none of them rang any bells for Frankie or Drew. Frankie was just about to give up when the trio came across a strange statue near the end of a corridor. It was a carving of a lion fighting a dragon.

'How cool is this statue?' said Drew. 'When I turn eighteen this will be my first tattoo.'

'It'll actually be your third,' Future Frankie whispered, much to Drew's delight.

'It'll actually be our way out,' Frankie said, grinning, as something clicked in his mind. 'There was a coat of arms of a lion fighting a dragon on Sir Trottsalot's cape, back at the jousting competition. So this must be it!' He gave the statue an experimental shove, expecting an escape hatch to open in the wall behind it, or even in the floor, but nothing happened.

'Try lifting it,' said Drew.

Frankie tried, but it was way too heavy. He rolled his eyes, realising Drew had pranked him – but as he did so, he saw a glimpse of something in the ceiling. 'Drew, lift your torch,' he said.

All three adventurers looked up, and all three could just see a circular slab of clay in the ceiling.

'A manhole!' said Future Frankie. 'Actually, it's called a person-hole in my timeline,' he corrected himself.

'Looks like the only way is up,' said Drew,

raising the torch a little higher. 'I've always said that.'

'How are we going to reach it?' Frankie asked.

'That's why God gave you shoulders, Frankie,' Drew said, slapping him on the back.

Frankie was taller than Drew, so he climbed onto his older self's shoulders and tried to push the manhole cover upwards. He **pushed** and **pushed**, but it didn't budge.

'Come on, Frankie, put some muscle behind it,' Drew shouted. Frankie heaved again; this time, the clay moved a tiny bit but then slammed back down as if someone was standing on it.

'I knew I should have done it,' cried Drew, 'it can't be *that* heavy!'

Frankie could usually take a joke, but the tension of the situation was getting to him and the ribbing he was receiving from Drew wasn't helping. He gritted his teeth and tried again.

'Come on, Frankie, once you open that cover we can get outside and get a signal, and then we are home sweet home,' Future Frankie said, trying to sound as encouraging as he could even though Frankie had kicked him twice in the chin and he knew for a fact there was more to come.

Frankie, fed up with the back-seat drivers below, took a deep breath. And then, with all his might, he hoisted the round slab of clay off its rim. Again, it bounced up and came straight back down.

Frankie repeated the tactic. This time he was able to clear half the hole.

'You got it, Frankie, just one more push!' yelled Drew.

Frankie pushed again and the lid popped out into the mud of the outside world.

'Yeah, Frankie! I never lost faith!' shouted Drew from below.

Frankie was able to hoist himself out. Future Frankie quickly gave Drew a boost up and then the two boys reached down and managed to pull Future Frankie out from the corridor and into the mud of the forest.

It wasn't until all three were out that they realised they were not alone, and Frankie quickly worked out why it had been so hard to push up the people-hole.

Not more than a few steps away was an **alligator** which was looking particularly **hungry**, and more than a little bit **angry**.

CHAPTER 21

SEE YA LATER, ALLIGATOR! (WE HOPE!)

'Stay perfectly still,' Future Frankie whispered.

This order was followed by his younger colleagues for a few beats; they had always been told that it was best to stay completely still if they were being attacked by a wild animal. But now, that seemed impossible. It was like being ordered to remain quiet during a tickle fight. A moment or two passed before Frankie uttered through gritted teeth, 'We can't stay perfectly still for the rest of our lives!'

'Just try for a bit longer,' said Future Frankie. 'On the count of three, I am going to engage Suity.'

It was like they were in a staring contest with a **dinosaur**. The alligator remained perfectly still except for its devious eyes, which shifted from one menu item to the other.

'OK, are we ready?' Future Frankie asked.

'What if it freaks it out and it leaps onto us?' asked his younger self.

'Well ... yes, that could happen,' he replied, which filled exactly nobody with confidence.

'One, two, three ... Suitcase engage!' Frankie Senior whispered into his wrist, and with that a light beamed from his watch before it leapt into the air and began spinning.

Frankie Junior kept his eyes firmly on the gator, which seemed transfixed by this latest development, its eyes widening, its grin becoming more guileful. Suity began to unravel from watch form into its traditional suitcase form, which appeared to spook the great reptile – but when a gator gets **spooked**, a gator **attacks**, and its tiny feet started taking tiny steps towards Suity. It occurred to Frankie then that the worst-case scenario might not be one of the humans getting eaten, but rather their lift home being devoured. If Suity disappeared down a gator's belly then, without a doubt, they would be stuck in the Middle Ages forever.

Drew would later swear he saw the great gator lick its lips before it leapt towards the spinning Sonic Suitcase, its jaws opened wide, its jagged teeth razor sharp.

The beast was airborne when Frankie shouted, 'Put your fingers in your ears!' and the sound of a whistle filled the night air. All of a sudden, the alligator was suspended in mid-air, its mouth as open as a 7-Eleven.

Future Frankie, still plugging his ears as best he could, looked to his side and saw the Stun

Whistle in the mouth of young Frankie Fish just as Suity fell into the mud, fully formed.

'Grabbed it before the guards dragged us away,' Frankie said with a wink.

'Nice one.' Future Frankie grinned, lowering his hands. 'Quickly, we have one minute. Let's go home before it wakes!' urged Frankie Senior. But, just before he was about to direct Suity to do exactly that, Frankie yelped.

'Wait! We need a **Circle of Safety**! I never forget that, not since what happened with the Vikings.'

'You're right,' Drew said, the blood draining from his face. 'Much as I would love to bring this gator back with us and make the Mosley triplets pee themselves, it may be more trouble than it's worth.'

The boys were right. The last time they hadn't implemented the Circle of Safety correctly – the only way to ensure that only selected participants came on a time-travel trip – they'd ended up with two Vikings wreaking havoc at St Monica's.

Future Frankie groaned. 'OK, OK,' he muttered, and began dragging his heel anti-clockwise through the mud. 'I'll create a circle.'

'You may want to hurry!' Frankie squirmed.

'Yes, I get it!' Future Frankie bellowed sarcastically. 'Do you think there's a **suspended alligator** I had forgotten about?'

'No, it's those knights charging towards us that have me a little concerned!' his younger self snapped back.

Future Frankie looked over his left shoulder to see three knights, presumably from the Brickenden clan, marching towards them with their swords drawn, screaming like they were keen on a battle.

For Frankie Fish, everything went into slow motion. The insanity of the moment hit him like a ton of bricks aboard a steam train. An alligator hung in mid-air, staring at him, while medieval knights charged towards them with swords that sparkled ominously in the moonlight.

The older version of himself was attempting a perfect circle in the mud in medieval England in order to fling them centuries into the future with his (their?) best friend, who had almost stayed behind to become a court jester in a castle. What a bizarre series of events had led Frankie here!

Time suddenly seemed to stop and, for some reason, Frankie thought of Scotland again. The three Grandads. The wet grass. The cold air. The grey clouds. *Grandad.* Grandad, who he hadn't hugged the last time he saw him. Then he saw the alligator lick his lips, felt a hand on his arm yank him into the Circle of Safety, and the last face he saw before time disappeared was his own.

CHAPTER 22

THE WORST DAY IN THE HISTORY OF THE WORLD

Frankie Fish arrived at St Monica's Primary alongside his best friend, Drew Bird. As he got his bearings, he glanced around, but there was no-one to be seen. No-one from his class, not a single Mosley triplet and not even that stickybeak Lisa Chadwick. Future Frankie had apparently returned to the, er, future. Frankie and Drew looked at each other, utterly clueless.

'Um, I know where we are, but ... what's going on?' Drew asked, completely baffled.

The silence was eerie.

Frankie knew *where* he was but not WHEN he was, as Suity could only approximate when to drop them off. And there was only one thing Frankie needed to know.

Without a word, and with a burst of speed rarely witnessed, he ran as hard as he could to Grandad and Nanna Fish's house. He ran so fast he felt like he was being carried by the wind – and, before he knew it, he was standing in his grandparents' driveway on a Saturday morning, watching Lou and Nanna holding each other, sobbing, on the front porch. An ambulance was heading off silently down the street.

Lou was sobbing. 'He's gone,' she sobbed in Nanna's arms. 'Grandad's really gone.'

And it was here that Frankie's heart broke for the very first time.

Everyone tried to make Frankie feel better about not being there when Grandad died, but nobody succeeded. He felt a sadness he had never felt before, and a regret so sharp it felt like he had swallowed a knife.

He wished he could go back to medieval England and try re-entering his own timeline with better co-ordinates, so he could time his rearrival better. But there was no Sonic Suitcase anymore. The original one had been reduced to ashes in a jousting pitch several hundred years into the past, and the new one was more than a decade away from being created by himself and Lou.

Yep, Frankie Fish was trapped. Right here, right now.

⚡

Grandad Fish's funeral was, unsurprisingly, sombre. Frankie's mum, Tina, asked if Frankie would like to say a prayer during mass, but he couldn't get the words out. Saint Lou finished it for him, holding his hand the whole time as he blubbered and shook.

Drew Bird attended the church service, as did his parents, as a show of support for their son's friend. It was all a bit of a blur for Frankie. He remembered his mum crying a lot, the hymns sung by Miss Merryweather, with Lisa Chadwick's mother on the organ, and the dried-out sandwiches at the afterparty, which Frankie's dad told him was called 'a wake'.

'Why do they call it a wake when somebody's dead?' Drew asked, trying to cheer his mate up.

'I think I need some time alone,' Frankie replied, and excused himself to the backyard of his grandad and nanna's house.

Frankie stood below low-hanging grey clouds, trying very hard not to cry. He felt like he hadn't had enough time with Grandad, or at least he had wasted too much time away from Grandad, and now it was all over. **Forever.** Just like that.

The Forbidden Shed loomed at the back of the garden among Nanna Fish's forget-me-nots, which were in bloom. Feeling drawn to the Forbidden Shed, Frankie slowly strolled over. The door was unlocked and, inside, it was obvious that Nanna Fish had done a bit of spring-cleaning. Grandad's photos, trophies and trinkets were all still there, but they had been dusted carefully. A vase of blue **forget-me-nots** on the Charging Bench – which was now actually just a bench – brightened up the room.

Frankie was still grappling with the thought that Grandad and the Sonic Suitcase were gone when, once again, he was drawn to something. He pulled open the bench's top drawer and, somehow, was both surprised and unsurprised to find a gift-wrapped box with an envelope attached that had his name on it. The box, like the drawer that housed it, was a decent size. You could easily store a football in it.

He gently took the box out of the drawer and placed it on the bench. 'Is this a birthday gift Grandad and Nanna forgot to give to me?' he wondered aloud. He decided he needed cheering up, so he tore the wrapping off the box and opened the lid.

Frankie lifted a helmet out of the box. It was a combination of a bike helmet and the kind of helmet Luke Skywalker wore during his lightsabre training. Frankie was pretty up-to-date with the latest video-game accessories, but this wasn't PlayStation-related; this looked more like a one-off, homemade contraption. In fact, it had a distinctly *Grandad* flair.

Hoping for some kind of explanation, Frankie ripped open the envelope and pulled out a card. On the front was a hand-drawn picture of forget-me-not flowers; inside were these shakily written words.

Frankie,

There is still time. There will always be time. Put the helmet on and press the red button on the left-hand side. Close your eyes and take a deep breath.

See you soon,
Grandad

Frankie's hands began to shake as he grabbed the helmet and threw it on his head. His fingers fumbled for the red button on the left side, then pressed it down. *Click.*

Nothing happened. Frankie read the card again; he had forgotten to close his eyes and take a deep breath. Frankie squeezed his eyes shut and filled his lungs with air. He took one deep breath, then another one. Then another. He felt his heartbeat slow. He felt calm. And then the most remarkable thing happened.

Frankie opened his eyes and he was no longer in the Forbidden Shed. He was standing on wet grass under grey clouds. The cold air pricked his cheeks. There was a huge boulder to his left. It felt like he'd only been here yesterday.

'It's a weird kind of deja vu, ain't it, kiddo?' came the throaty but friendly voice of Grandad before the old man appeared from behind the boulder.

'**Grandad!**' Frankie bellowed with joy, as he drank in the sight of him. 'What happened? Where are we? Did you even *die?*'

'It sure seems like it,' Grandad said. 'Because I sure as hell know ye wouldn't have gone in me shed to get that helmet without permission if I was still alive!' His eyes sparkled merrily.

Frankie gestured around at the endless green rolling hills. 'Are we in **heaven**?'

Grandad rolled his eyes good-naturedly. 'No, ye dimwit! Before I died, I made us a protected time-loop where we can visit each other sometimes. It took a lot of work, but it's out of the normal timeline, so it'll always just be me, ye and Lou if she wants to visit occasionally. And it'll be wiped after every visit, so ye can come whenever ye want without running into yerself. What a disaster that'd be, eh?'

Frankie couldn't speak. His throat felt like it was full of balloons, and he didn't know whether to laugh, cry or shout. He felt like he'd won the lottery.

Grandad chuckled. 'I always knew there was a chance ye would miss saying goodbye, with all yer misadventure,' he added, 'so I wanted to make sure we had our own space and time.'

'But how?' Frankie marvelled, finally finding his voice again. 'This is **incredible**.'

'Oh, I'll tell ye one day. We have plenty of time for that. Now, tell me all about yer trip to meet Uncle Arthur. Did ye get the Chalice of Flames?'

Frankie hung his head. 'It got burnt to a crisp at a jousting match,' he said, 'and it was my fault. I'm really sorry I can't show it to you, Grandad.'

'It doesn't matter,' Grandad replied. 'I'd much rather see you anyway. So did ye like the helmet? I always liked the idea of using a watch for travel, but maybe that's something for ye to think about in the future …'

As Alfie Fish spoke, Frankie felt the urge to hug his grandad. And this time, he didn't ignore it.

He leapt at the old man, flung his arms around him, and hugged him tighter than he'd ever hugged anyone. '**I love you, Grandad.**'

'I love ye too, kiddo,' Grandad said, sounding a bit choked up. He put his arm around his one and only favourite grandson and whispered, 'No-one's ever really gone.'

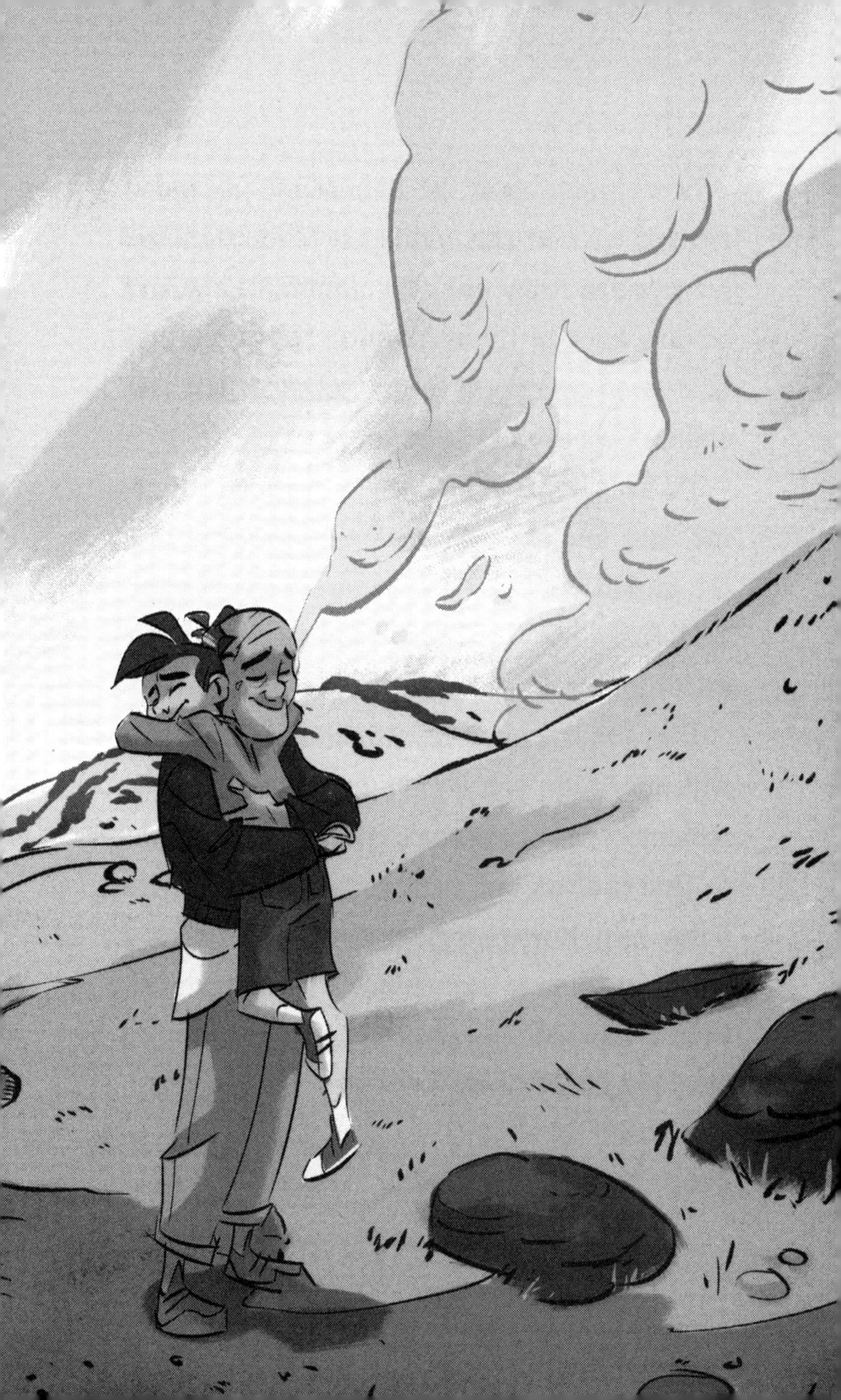

When Frankie took the helmet off, he found himself back in the Forbidden Shed. He knew his grandad really *had* died, and that he wasn't coming back in the real world, but he felt like he'd been given the most precious gift. He couldn't wait to tell Saint Lou.

He bent down to pick one of Nanna's forget-me-nots, and as he did his mum came out into the garden. 'How are you doing, sweetie?' asked Tina Fish (aka Tuna Fish) tenderly. 'You must miss him terribly. I know you were close.'

'I'm OK,' Frankie replied, smiling at her. 'I will miss him, you know? But as long as you remember them, no-one's ever really gone.'

Tina sniffled, and then gathered her son into a hug (yep, it was a big day for hugs). 'That is a very wise thing to say, Francis,' she murmured. After a moment, she pulled back, wiped away a tear, and gave Frankie a watery smile.

'I meant to tell you,' she said, 'I was talking to Drew's parents and they've invited you to their holiday house for a week during the summer holidays. Now, I know how devastated you were when you missed out on going on last year's trip because of that silly prank you two played with the proposal banner,' she added with a groan, trying to repress the memory of that day's fallout, 'but you have been such a good boy this year. And you seem happier, too. So, how does a week at the beach with the Birds sound?'

'Finally!' Frankie squealed.

Tina couldn't help but giggle at Frankie's reaction. It was a little bit of sunshine on a sad day.

'Can you believe you were suspended a year ago?' she said, shaking her head. 'So much has happened since then.'

Frankie grinned at her. 'Tell me about it,' he said. 'So, so much!'

CHAPTER 23

SHOW AND DON'T TELL

Frankie and Drew couldn't wait to dash off to the beach together, but they needed to get through one more day of school before the summer holidays. Just one day. No pranks. Good behaviour.

'May I just say how pleased I am at how much thought you have all put into your family history presentations,' Miss Merryweather said that Friday morning. 'Well, everyone but the Mosley triplets and their jar of farts, but let's not give that any more thought than it deserves,' she muttered, almost gagging at the memory. 'So now, our last family Show and Tell will be none other than Francis Fish!' Miss Merryweather attempted to get some applause going, but the gesture was only reciprocated by Drew Bird.

Frankie nervously rose from his desk and walked to the dreaded front of the class, carrying an old sports bag with him.

'Good luck, Fish Guts,' Lisa Chadwick snickered under her breath, but Drew gave him a supportive thumbs up.

Frankie turned and faced the class, but felt frozen to the spot. Sensing a firm case of **stage fright**, Miss Merryweather prompted him. 'Would you like to tell us what you have for us today, Francis?'

'It's an ugly old sports bag, a-ma-zing!' Lisa Chadwick whispered, getting a few titters from her besties in the second row.

Frankie took a deep breath and forced himself to speak. 'I have something that means a lot to my family and to me,' he said, reaching into his bag and producing a hook.

The class suddenly sat up straight and oohed and aahed. It even got the Mosley triplets' attention ('Are you related to a pirate?' one of them said).

'This was my grandad's hook,' Frankie said slowly. 'His name was Alfie Fish and he passed away recently.'

Unusually, the class had fallen silent – so quiet you could hear a pin drop onto a puff of fairy floss.

'I wanted to tell you about his hook,' he went on, 'because in its own weird way this hook was the reason my grandad became my grandad.' Frankie couldn't take his eyes off the hook, but the class was so quiet that he soon looked up. He was stunned to see they were all leaning forward like they actually wanted to hear the story about the old man with the hook for a hand. Even Lisa Chadwick was staring at him.

Frankie cleared his throat and kept talking.

He hadn't really rehearsed this, but he knew perfectly well where the story actually started. 'You could say our family only exists because way back in 1952 in Scotland, my grandad, Alfie Fish, drove against Clancy Fairplay in the Big Race and nearly died.'

From there, Frankie told the class everything. How Grandad had crashed in the Big Race and lost his hand, and how a nurse called Mavis Hopley had nursed him back to health and fallen in love with him. How Grandad's rival, Clancy Fairplay, tried to steal Mavis's affections away – and how Grandad and Mavis went on a date at a theatre, to see the Amazing Freido, which sealed their fate. He spoke for what felt like a long time, and Miss Merryweather didn't interrupt him.

But Frankie didn't stop there. He told them about Grandad's time-travelling suitcase, and how he himself, with his friend Drew Bird, had rescued Grandad and Nanna from a prison in Imperial China. How close they came to

Armageddon when they were followed back from Norway by a pair of Viking siblings. He talked about their visit to the Academy in Ancient Greece and Saint Lou's appearance at the first Olympics. The way they'd met Laughing Sparrow in the Wild West. Their Egyptian tomb-raiding. And, of course, that time they saw a pig compete in a jousting contest.

'You can take our pride, but you'll never take our Bacon!' Drew shouted, and the class erupted in cheers, hooting and hollering – even Miss Merryweather laughed.

The lunchtime bell rang, but no-one moved a muscle. Then Miss Merryweather asked, 'How does the story end, Francis?'

'I don't know yet, Miss,' Frankie replied. 'But what I do know is that, as long as you remember them, no-one is ever really gone.' He put Alfie's hook back in the old sports bag and walked happily to his seat, giving Drew a fist bump on the way through.

⚡

At lunchtime, Frankie was sitting outside with Drew when he looked up to see his nemesis standing in front of him. *Oh great*, he thought. *What does Lisa Chadwick want now?*

'I know almost everything you said was made up,' she began, 'but my favourite aunty passed away earlier this year, and ... well, what you said about nobody ever really being gone, do you believe that?'

Frankie wasn't sure if he was being tested, but he was sure that Lisa Chadwick seemed different somehow. She wasn't being a plain old stickybeaking pain in the neck. She was being sincere, and even vulnerable.

So Frankie looked her in the eye and said: 'No, I don't believe it.'

'Oh,' Lisa responded, disappointed.

'I know it,' Frankie added with

a reassuring smile, and it must have been contagious, because Lisa Chadwick was **smiling** back at him.

Frankie felt a little giddy all of a sudden. He couldn't believe he'd made Lisa Chadwick smile.

'You should tell the truth more often, Frankie Fish,' she said, 'and maybe one day, if you like, we could go to the Cocoa Pit together and have a hot chocolate with marshmallows.'

Frankie heard the word 'sure' flying out of his mouth like a bat out of a haunted cave before turning to see Drew staring.

At the same moment, Frankie remembered his future self telling him: 'You won't believe who you marry!'

Good Lord, Frankie thought suddenly. *Do I marry Lisa Chadwick??*

CHAPTER 24

FINALLY! THE BEACH!

Frisbees, salt water and beach cricket.

Frankie was finally on holiday with his best and only mate, Drew Bird. They had eaten ice-cream every day and laughed like hyenas in a tickling contest.

One day, as they threw tennis balls to each other in waist-deep water, diving to take 'Classic Catches' and getting dunked under the waves, something occurred to Drew.

'Hey Frankie, I have a question for you.'

'How am I so much better at taking catches than you?'

'Haha, you wish!' Drew grinned, before looking serious again. 'When we were back in my quarters in Farthington's Castle, and I told you I wasn't coming back ...'

'Yeah? Worst decision ever, by the way.'

'... you and Future Frankie told Suity to take you home,' Drew recalled, catching a ball and holding it for a moment.

Frankie shrugged. 'Well, I wasn't going to hang out in the Middle Ages forever.'

'Sure,' said Drew suspiciously, like he was putting a rude puzzle together. 'But later on, when we saw the alligator, you said you **NEVER** forget the Circle of Safety since the Vikings kerfuffle.'

'Ye-es ...'

'And yet you didn't have a Circle of Safety set up within my bedroom at Lord Farthington's

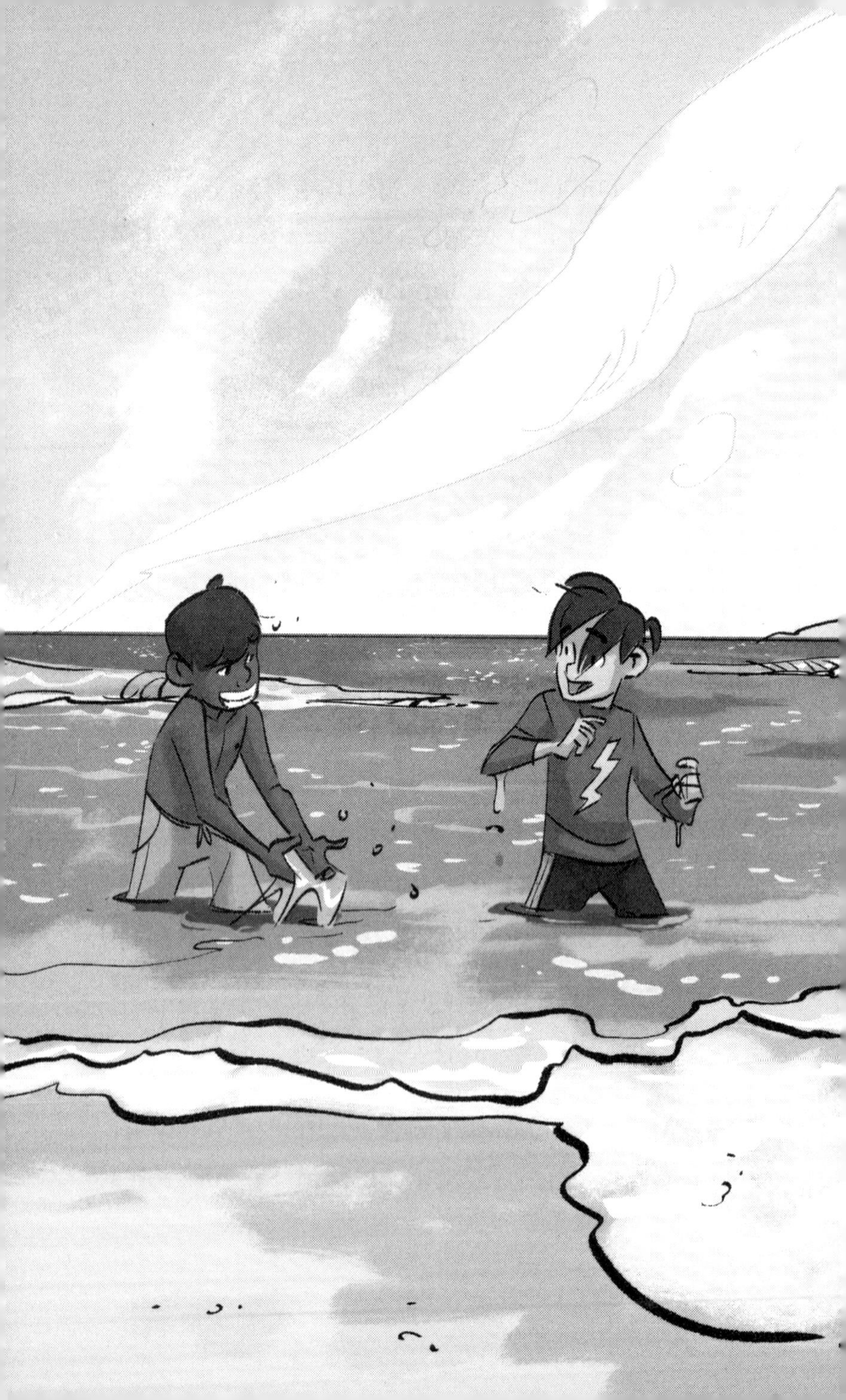

castle,' Drew prompted. He threw the ball back at Frankie. 'Which means ...'

Frankie let the tennis ball whizz past his head and laughed.

'It means you would have been dragged back home with us anyway.'

Drew snorted. 'You cheeky bugger!'

'I was never going to lose my one and only **best friend**, Drew Bird,' Frankie said, splashing him.

Drew clapped his hands. 'Thank you, Frankie Fish. Thank you.'

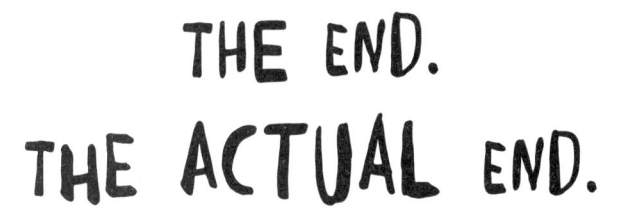

THE END.
THE ACTUAL END.

AUTHOR'S NOTE

Frankie Fish went on to write stories about time-travelling with his grandfather. Nobody believed they were true, so they were considered 'fiction'. To protect his privacy, he published his first book, The Sonic Suitcase, under the pseudonym Peter Helliar.

I told you this was autobiographical!

ABOUT THE AUTHOR

Peter Helliar is the best-selling author of the *Frankie Fish* series and one of Australia's favourite comedians. He lives in Melbourne with his wife and three kids.

The Gold Logie nominee co-hosts the award-winning news and current affairs program *The Project*, and wrote and starred in the new TV comedy *How To Stay Married*, both on Network Ten. His latest family comedy show is *The Complete History of Better Books*. He plans to interview Frankie Fish on *The Project* one day, in what will hopefully be an exclusive.

ACKNOWLEDGEMENTS

What an amazing journey this has been! Firstly, I want to thank all the kids who have taken Frankie, Drew, Saint Lou and Grandad and the whole gang into their hearts and homes. Receiving pictures of you dressing up for Book Week as Frankie (and other members of the gang!) makes my heart leap every time.

Thank you to the mums and dads, grandparents, aunts and uncles and, of course, librarians and booksellers who put Frankie Fish into the hands of your loved ones. I am indebted.

To Marisa Pintado, thank you so much for organising a coffee over five years ago and for not only believing in Frankie but taking such beautiful care of him.

To the entire Hardie Grant Children's Publishing team: Luna Soo, Penelope White, Kristy Lund-White, Amanda Shaw, Johanna Gogos and all the sales team who work so hard to get Frankie out into the world!

Lesley Vamos, thank you for merging our imaginations and bringing Frankie and team to life. I will miss the giddiness of seeing your latest illustrations for the first time.

My agents, team and friends at Token Artists: firstly, Dioni Andis, who knows when I have twenty seconds to speak or twenty minutes to chat, and tolerates both! Kevin Whyte, Helen Townshend, Kathleen McCarthy, Sam Gray, Rowan Smith, Charlie Falkner. Thanks for the guidance and support.

Mum, Dad, Mark, Karen (there are great Karens out there!), Rachel, Lisa, Rod, Annette, Mitch, Olivia, Ally and Will. Family always.

Of course, my gang: Brij, Liam, Aidan and Oscar. I'm super proud and thrilled to be travelling through time with all of you.

So – off the next adventure. I hope you come along for the ride! It'll be fun. I promise!

Pete

PSSST!

WANNA LEARN HOW TO DO SOME OF FRANKIE AND DREW'S

FAVOURITE PRANKS?

THEN READ ON!

NEVER LET SLEEPING SUCKERS LIE!

TWO IN THE BED: Make a human (or ALIEN!) head out of papier-mâché and paint. Remember to keep this a SECRET, until you're ready to slip it into your prankee's bed next to them while they're sleeping!

PERFECT FOR SLEEPOVERS!

BUGBRAINED: Cut out some silhouettes of bugs from black paper. Stick 'em to the inside of the bedside lamps and make sure the lamps are turned off, for maximum prank effectiveness when a sucker turns them back on!

SNOOZE BUTTON: Hide alarms all over the bedroom — and the house!

PRO TIP

Set them to go off five minutes after each other — once the prankee finds the last, the next will start!

PRO TIP: Wear socks and tiptoe around so that you don't wake your prankee. Not only will you LOOK the part, but there's a reason King Kong was a terrible prankster – you could hear him coming from miles away!

POP-A-PALOOZA: Fill the bedroom with balloons. ALL THE BALLOONS!

BUTT-DIAL: Change the sleeping prankee's phone alarm to supersonic fart noises.

NIAGARA FALLS: Fill the bedroom with plastic cups of water, set up **SUPER**-close to each other, so the prankee can't leave the bed without **WETTING** themselves! You'll need to be EXTRA careful not to prank yourself when you're setting this up!

OVERNIGHT ARRIVAL: Put a chair in the room and sit up some clothes stuffed with newspapers to look like a person. For the head, take a balloon and stick a printed-out face on it (of someone like your **favourite** author, Peter Helliar).

THE MOST IMPORTANT MEAL OF THE DAY: BREAKFAST PRANKS

A prank-tastic way to start the day!

UDDERLY DISGUSTING: Scatter green jelly crystals in all the cereal packets. When the prankee adds milk, they'll turn GREEN with disgust!

SOURPUSS: To turn breakfast really **sour**, add lemon juice to the orange juice.

SWEET AND SALTY: Offer to make Nutella on toast for everyone. Spread a thick layer of Vegemite underneath, and top it with Nutella!

DINNER FOR BREAKFAST: Replace the orange juice with water, then sprinkle in cheese powder.

BAD EGGS: Sneak out the carton of eggs, and carefully prick a hole in the bottom of each egg with a pin. Drain the eggs' insides and hide the liquid in a container in the back of the fridge. Then put back the carton and watch confusion reign!

FRO-YO: The night before, pour your mum's muesli into a bowl, add yoghurt and freeze the whole lot. Offer to make her breakfast in bed, and watch her spoon bend!

CEREAL OFFENDER: Swap the bags of cereal around in their cardboard boxes, so that whoever opens the Rice Bubbles box will find Corn Flakes ... and whoever opens the Corn Flakes box finds muesli! Swap them around every day to be a **REAL** cereal offender!

SEVEN DAYS A WEEK: Pretend that it's Monday on Sunday. Get up early, get dressed for school, and run into your parents' room screaming, 'WE'RE LATE FOR SCHOOL!' See how close you can get to school before they smell a prank!

> **PRO TIP**
> Rope your siblings in for this one – it'll help sell the prank!

TREAT 'EM MEAN, KEEP 'EM CLEAN: BATHROOM PRANKS

NO SCRUBS: Paint a bar of soap with clear nail polish. Let it dry completely, then put it back in the shower. The prankee will spend hours trying to get foamy!

PUDDLE-O-PEE: Lift the seat and wrap plastic wrap over the toilet bowl. [Warning: this will really *pee* people off.]

PILE-O-POOP: Leave a fake poo on the floor.

PILE-O-POOP-PAPER: Stack all the toilet paper rolls in a very precarious stack, and hide the on-the-go roll. You could use short sticks to connect some of the rolls, so that when the prankee takes a roll, they will all fall!

HELLO FROM THE OTHER SIDE: When the bathroom mirror's all fogged up after your shower, use your finger to write 'HELP ME' in the steam. The next person to fog up the mirror will see the message — and think they're being haunted!

POWDER PUFF: Dust talcum powder in the nozzle of the hair dryer. When it's turned on, your prankee's hair will turn grey!

I'M WATCHING YOU: Put googly eyes on every container in the bathroom.

NINE OUT OF TEN DENTISTS RECOMMEND: Fill an empty toothpaste tube using a squeezy bottle of mayonnaise, and put it back in the bathroom — then run for cover!

PRANK KING

SPOTLIGHT:
TOILET PAPER PRANKS

- Hide a black pen in the bathroom. Every time you're in there, draw a spider on the other side of the on-the-go roll.

- Replace the on-the-go roll with a roll of 'toilet paper' made of:
  - Cellophane
  - Newspaper
  - Post-It Notes
  - Masking tape

Remember to put the ACTUAL toilet paper somewhere near the toilet, so whoever uses the toilet knows it's just a prank. Otherwise, you'll be in DEEP POOP!

FAST PRANKS FOR SIBLINGS

TEEN IDOL: Just before her friends come over, replace all your sister's bedroom posters with posters of the **daggiest** pop star in the world.

POP-THE-PANTS: Place some money on the floor, and stand out of sight. When your brother leans down to pick up the money, rip a piece of material. He'll be looking for the rip in his pants all day!

POP-A-PALOOZA 2.0: Ease all of their small or flexible belongings into balloons, then blow them up. Just be careful not to snag any holes in the rubber!

THE DAILY NEWS: Sign them up to news alerts for their **least** favourite movie star.

PRO TIP

Set their alert notification sound to a recording of someone saying, 'GOTCHA!'

90% OFF: Put a **FOR SALE** sign in the front yard — with your sister's face on it.

FINDING NEMO: Glue some googly eyes on a baby carrot. Put it in your brother's fish tank.

IT'S GOT LEGS: Run into their room with an empty container and shout **'LOOK AT THIS HUGE SPIDER I CAUGHT!'** then 'accidentally' drop the container on their bed — with the lid off!

FOUR-EYES: Put googly eyes on all the photos of them in the house.

EAR-WORM: Quietly play 'This Is The Song That Never Ends' outside their bedroom door every morning — it will be stuck in their head for weeks!

BRAIN-FART: Put a whoopee cushion under their pillow.

> Slide the whoopee cushion under their fitted sheet, so that they don't see it until they **HEAR** it!

PRO TIP

PLAY WITH YOUR FOOD!

Better yet, play with someone else's!

ICY CRAWLIES: Freeze fake insects into your ice cubes.

PRO TIP

If you use hot water the ice will set clearer, so it will be super easy to see the insect!

MINTY FRESH: Scrape out the middle of an Oreo and replace the filling with toothpaste!

ARE YOU READY FOR THIS JELLY?: Use yellow jelly to encase your prankee's favourite **hard** thing. Staplers, ceramic trinkets and yoyos are all perfect!

PRO TIP

It works best if you let one layer of jelly set, then put the prop on top, then pour another layer over it.

EAT IT: Pour orange jelly into glasses, and add a straw to each. Once it's set, offer everyone glasses of 'cordial'!

PERFECT FOR PARTIES

CAKE BURGER: Use food dye to make a layered cake that looks like a hamburger — and offer it to your dad!

PRO TIP Use cream for the mayonnaise!

SWEET SURPRISE: Swap the table salt for sugar!

ICE-CREAM POTATO: Use mashed potato to make an 'ice-cream sundae' for your sister.

PRO TIP Use gravy for the chocolate sauce!

TRUFFLE PIG: Cover brussels sprouts in melted chocolate. Chocolate truffle, anyone?

MAKE SOME NOISE

Pranks for when things are JUST TOO QUIET!

HONK HONK

1. Attach a harmonica to the front grille of your dad's car with some tape.
2. Once the car goes over 60 km/hour, the harmonica will start honking!

HONNNNNNNNK

1. Tape an airhorn to the back of a doorhandle so the button is facing the wall.
2. Once the door is opened and hits the wall, the airhorn will go **off**.

ANTI GIGGLES TIP

Set up all these pranks using only one hand — not the hand you use to write with. It'll take so much concentration you'll be distracted from giggling.

POP POP

1. When you're home alone, tape lots of inflated balloons to the wall behind the front door (if it opens inwards).
2. Close the door, and when someone else comes home and opens it, the balloons will **POP!**

POPPPPPPPPP!

1. Record the sound of microwave popcorn **popping** on your phone.
2. Play it at opportune times, like the quiet scenes in scary movies!

NOISE ANNOYS

1. De-tune a radio so it's playing distorted, scratchy music.
2. Hide it somewhere in the house and watch it drive everyone **nuts!**

HIGH-TECH HIJINKS!

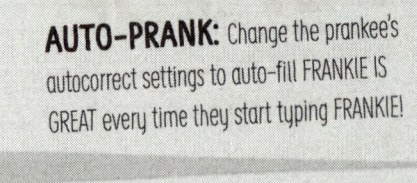

AUTO-PRANK: Change the prankee's autocorrect settings to auto-fill FRANKIE IS GREAT every time they start typing FRANKIE!

TOUCH-TYPING: Very carefully lift off the keys from the computer keyboard. Put them back in the wrong order!

PRO TIP: If your grandad has an awesome **Sonic Suitcase** like Frankie's does, this can be an excellent pranking tool. Just make sure you don't disrupt the timeline like the old cranky-pants nearly did in Scotland, 1952! And always make sure your battery is fully charged **BEFORE** you attempt a high-tech prank!

MOUSETRAP: Cover the laser in the bottom of the computer mouse with tape — the suckers will never know!

PRANK CALLING: Personalise the ringtones on the prankee's phone so that each person in the address book has their own ringtone. Obviously, you should go for funny noises — so that if your dad calls your mum, your mum's phone will make a farting sound!

ERROR, ERROR: Take a screenshot of the prankee's computer desktop, then add an error message on top of the image. Replace this as the computer background!

LONG-LOST BROTHER: One by one, take every family photo in your house, scan it, add a picture of your favourite author **EVER** — Peter Helliar — into it, and then print it out and slide it in over the original photograph. This is a slow burn, but when someone finally notices the newest member of the family, the pay-off will be GLORIOUS!

QUIZMASTER: If your TV can record shows, save one of your family's favourite quiz shows and memorise all the answers. Then you can sneakily put it on next time your family is watching together — they'll be amazed at how many answers you get right!

PRO TIP

Take bets on how many answers you know — and watch as the money rolls in!

COPYCAT

A classic that will test any prankster's commitment to the prank!

PRANK PREPARATION

During the week prior, sneak clothing from your sibling's clean laundry. You'll need a full outfit for the prank. Sneaking it all at once can be too obvious. Make notes about their daily routines so you can copy them.

> **PRO TIP**: If they wear glasses and you don't, make these from pipecleaners.

PRANK DAY

Set your alarm for the same time as your sibling. Dress in their clothes and arrive in the kitchen just prior to them. Eat the same breakfast, say the same sentences. BECOME THEM. **Follow them to school, to their locker, to their classroom. DO NOT LOSE THEM.**

> **PRO TIP**: For maximum impact, walk one step behind them at all times.

Their teacher will likely take their side, so ensure you are ready for recess and lunchtime. You must run from your class to shadow your sibling for the entire break. When questioned, claim that you're just trying to learn how to be as funny as they are.

> **PRO TIP:** Enlist their friends in the prank. Sit with them at recess and lunch, and only answer to your sibling's name.

Follow them to their after-school activities. **DO NOT BREAK CHARACTER.**

> **PRO TIP:** Go one step further, and beat your sibling to every event. Replace them on the sports field. Sit in their chair. Sleep in their bed.

POST PRANK

Pretend nothing happened.

CLASSIC PRANKS
FOR A PARTY CROWD

TOOT TIME: Put a whoopee cushion on someone's chair or in their back pocket!

PRO TIP
More than one whoopee cushion at a party makes for a carefully timed orchestra of toots.

PARTY POPPER: Tape a party popper onto the toilet door while someone's inside, so that when they leave they get a POPPER of a surprise.

HOLEY-MOLEY: Put a glass of straws on the table, but don't tell anyone that you've pricked them all with a sewing pin. Serving drinks has never been so fun — or so messy, so do this one in a room that has tiles, not carpet, for a quick clean-up!

BRING-A-PAVLOVA: Cover an upside-down ice-cream container with shaving cream and candles.

BRING-A-SPONGE CAKE: Cover a big sponge (like the one you use to wash the car) with icing sugar and candles.

BROWN-E's: Print and cut out lots of brown letter E's. Place them on a baking tray and cover them with foil, then announce to the party that you've brought a tray of brownies!

YOU'RE PRESENT ENOUGH: Rope the whole party in, and have everyone come dressed in costume as the birthday boy or girl!

COST-U-OR-ME: Tell only ONE GUEST that it's a costume party!

PIN THE TAIL ON THE SUPER-LOUD DONKEY: Set up a traditional game of pin the tail on the donkey. Make sure the tails are attached to pins or thumbtacks. When it's the birthday person's turn, hold balloons in front of the donkey for a game that ends in a BANG!

SEASON'S PRANKINGS!

EGG-CELLENT PRANKS FOR EASTER

Any day's a good day for a prank, but special occasions call for special-occasion pranks!

Wrap everyone's eggs in several more layers of foil.

Leave rabbit poop trails (chocolate bullets) all over the house.

Host an Easter egg hunt but don't hide any eggs. Or use real eggs instead of chocolate ones!

Have an egg-and-spoon race but don't hard-boil the eggs. SMASH!

Take a bite out of everyone's eggs and rewrap them.

Wrap up brussels sprouts so they look like Easter eggs, and generously leave piles of them around the house, or in your classroom.

HO-HO-HILARIOUS
PRANKS FOR CHRISTMAS

Hide all the presents and fill everyone's Christmas stockings with rocks.

Leave reindeer poop (Maltesers) all over the house.

Dress up as Santa and pretend to have fallen asleep on the couch.

Wrap yourself up as a present and wait under the tree. When someone approaches, jump out at them!

Add a pile of fake presents to the pile of real presents. Wrap up things you can easily find around the house — like dirty laundry, cans of dog food and rolls of toilet paper — and place them under the tree. Remember to place a gift tag on each one so they look genuine.

If it snows where you live, put on your warmest and most waterproof outfit, and have your pranking pal cover you in snow to become a snowman — then wait for the perfect moment, and BUST out to scare a passer-by.

Replace the presents with carefully gift-wrapped cardboard boxes.

BOOK ONE

BOOK TWO

BOOK THREE

BOOK FOUR

AUSTRALIA READS SPECIAL EDITION

BOOK FIVE

BOOK SIX

Have you read ALL of Frankie Fish's time-travel adventures?